Home for Christmas

also by John Forrest

Angels, Stars and Trees
Tales of Christmas Magic
(Scrivener, 2007)

Home for Christmas

A Family Saga of Rural Canada

John Forrest

Library and Archives Canada Cataloguing in Publication

Forrest, John.
Home for Christmas : a family saga of rural Canada / John Forrest.

Short stories.
ISBN 978-1-896350-55-4

1. Christmas stories, Canadian (English). I. Title.

PS8611.O772H64 2012 C813'.6 C2012-904770-8

Book design: Laurence Steven
Cover design and interior illustrations: Chantal Bennett

Published by Scrivener Press
465 Loach's Road,
Sudbury, Ontario, Canada, P3E 2R2
info@yourscrivenerpress.com
www.scrivenerpress.com

We acknowledge the financial support of the Ontario Arts Council, the Canada Council for the Arts and the Government of Canada through the Canada Book Fund for our publishing activities.

ONTARIO ARTS COUNCIL
CONSEIL DES ARTS DE L'ONTARIO
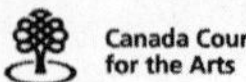
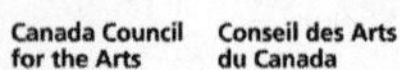

Acknowledgements

Although I write the words, I could not have achieved the storytelling success I have had without the help of others. I deeply appreciate the inspiration, guidance and support of those listed below.

Carol Forrest, Rob Forrest, Dana Forrest, Meada and Jim Hunter, Ann and John Locke, Lloyd Dennis, Betty Hard, Randy Lucenti, Julie Langpeter, Mark Bisset, Johanna Powell, Laurence and Jan Steven, Marylynne White, Home Hardware Orillia, Home Hardware Canada, *The Orillia Packet and Times*, the Mariposa Writers Group, *Lake Simcoe Living Magazine*, the Washago Seniors and the Ontario Arts Council

Dedication

To my beloved wife, my "Christmas Carol," whose guidance, encouragement and love have inspired and supported me in all my endeavours, and who truly is the "magic" in my life.

Table of Contents

Foreword

Christmas is a time for family get-togethers, decking the halls, lighting the tree, good food, giddy children, renewing friendships and many other traditions. For Simcoe County readers an anxiously awaited tradition, established a decade ago, is Orillia author John Forrest's annual Christmas serial. John's smooth delivery of family-based stories allows for the readers to become a part of the plots, whether through reminiscing about similar situations in their own lives or by simply drifting into the lives of the characters he so aptly creates. *Home for Christmas* is a collection of five of those stories which chronicle the yuletide adventures, challenges and triumphs of the Stone family. You will enjoy them. John is a literary treasure and we are fortunate to share in his writings.

Randy Lucenti
Regional Managing Editor, North Central Ontario
Sun Media, June 2012

Preface

Dear Reader,

Thank you for choosing *Home For Christmas*. I hope you enjoy the stories and that each leaves you filled with the joy and spirit of Christmas and a renewed appreciation of why it exists.

I began writing short stories to share recollections of the exceptional events and wonderful people who have touched my very full life. My happy childhood, an exciting and interesting thirty five year career in education and my role as husband and father provided me with a rich source of material. In particular the celebration of Christmas holds many cherished memories in our family, and my first anthology *Angels Stars and Trees: Tales of Christmas Magic* was written to celebrate, share and preserve actual events in my life, or those of people dear to me.

The stories in *Home For Christmas* are not a sequel to *Angels Stars and Trees*. Rather, they represent a new and exciting stage in my growth as a writer, as I venture into the realm of historical fiction. The varied settings and time periods of the first half of the twentieth century are accurate and many of the characters are based on real people from that era, but the Stone family and their stories are fictional.

Though each story in *Home For Christmas* stands on its own, the events chronicled from the Stones' lives are placed in chronological order. I recommend you begin your reading with "Becca's Star," which introduces the background and sets the stage for the tales that follow.

May I add that the stories were written to be read aloud as well as enjoyed privately, and that it is my sincere hope that their telling will prompt you to recall and share your cherished Christmas memories. Enjoy the read and may the spirit and magic of this most special season forever touch the lives of you and yours.

Merry Christmas!

JF

Orillia, July 2012

Becca's Star

Mary Stone stood by the kitchen window gazing at the winter wonderland spread before her. How could something so powerful and frightening in the night, leave such beauty in its wake?

Last night's storm had clothed the drive-yard in an unblemished coat of snow. The fence posts surrounding it were wrapped in drifted scarves of white and capped with matching top hats. Beyond the fence, the front forty had been frosted with swirls of icing and sprinkled with a diamond glaze. There was no doubt; it would be a white Christmas!

She heard the horses before she saw them. Their whinnies, the jingle and slap of harness and her husband David's sharp commands announced the team's arrival from the driveshed. He and their son Paul appeared first, each leading a magnificent Clydesdale. The matched team of Atlas and Hercules was pulling the sleigh and their daughter Becca stood tall on the front deck, holding the reins. Shep, their border collie, provided an escort, bouncing up and down on his hind legs, pawing the air, eager to be included in the fun.

Given it was the dirty thirties, 1934 had been a good year for the Stone family. The past few years had been difficult, but it seemed the worst was over. This Christmas would mark their fifth on the farm.

The market crash of 1929 had cost David his job in Toronto. Mary and David, with ten year old Paul, and Rebecca, just seven, had returned to the rural Ontario community of Udney where she and David had been raised, to move in with Dave's parents Ben and Emily, on the Stone family farm. Situated east of Orillia, Udney was a typical central Ontario farm village. The Canadian Pacific Railway station at the crossroads, the United Church and Orange Hall were the focal points for the fifty or so family farms in the area.

The post crash economic depression brought poverty and despair to the land. But as mixed farmers they were mostly self-sufficient and there was always food on the table. However, there was barely enough cash money to buy breeding stock, seed, and fuel, or to repair existing machinery, and there was no money for anything new. The work was hard and the hours long, but Mary and Dave found returning to their roots to be satisfying. The children thrived and life was good.

Then in the winter of 1931 their family was touched by tragedy. Ben and Emily fell ill with a virulent strain of influenza and died at home, within hours of each other. The close knit community mourned its loss, but rural life waits for no one. Despite their grief the Stones carried on.

It had not been easy. Even though Mary and Dave came from farm backgrounds, the loss of his parents' knowledge, skill and willing hands was difficult to replace. However, despite the poor economic conditions, they were able to make a go of it. They had a solid roof over their heads, good food to eat and enough cream, milk, cash crop and livestock sales to provide a little extra. Each year things had gotten a bit better. Fewer transients looking for food and work dropped off the passing trains that ran the nearby rails, and Government "works" projects brought better roads and some modern conveniences.

The "Bell" telephone line reached their community in 1932. Mary glanced at the wooden telephone box mounted on the wall behind her. As if on cue, it rang to life. One short, two long; that would be the Hunters. There were now twenty-three families on the party line in the community and there would be more added before the new switchboard was installed in Brechin. Better communication was a great convenience, but not a necessity. Then finally, a year ago, they got electricity. The same poles that carried the telephone line now carried electric power from the new Swift Rapids hydro project right to the farm. But with cash in short supply the Stone family used this boon sparingly. Their first priority had been lighting. The farm house, barn and some out buildings now had electric lights. No more coal oil lamps, candles, lanterns, wick trimming, glass cleaning and refilling, and best of all, less danger of fire. The bright farm safety light atop the tall pole in the drive-yard now shone as a beacon of hope, even on the darkest night. This year their Christmas present to themselves was an electric pump for the well and the indoor plumbing fixtures to go with it. Soon there would be no more trips to the "little house outback;" chamber pots would become a thing of the past and she could have a real bath!

Perhaps someday they might afford an electric stove, but for now her trusty McClary four burner wood stove would continue to serve for both cooking and heating.

Their one luxury was the radio. It was their ear to the world. They listened daily to the weather, news and agricultural reports and planned their activities accordingly. At night, when the day's work was done and supper was finished, they tuned in to their favourite radio plays and of course Saturday night was set aside for Foster Hewitt's play-by-play account of the Toronto Maple Leaf hockey games. Yes, they were a fortunate family and she was a happy woman, blessed with a hard working, caring husband, two fine children and a good life in a close knit community.

Her musing was interrupted by David's call from the yard.

"Mary, we're ready to leave!"

She dried her hands on her apron, picked up the bundle she had prepared for delivery to David's bachelor brother Bill, hurried to the back door and stepped out on to the porch. It was cold!

The horses were snorting steam from their flared nostrils as they tossed their heads in eager anticipation and it billowed in the frigid air above them. David and Paul were now perched on the driver's seat of the sleigh and Becca was dancing up and down on the ground beside her father, begging to be included on the trip. But he denied her. They would have a large enough load as it was and besides she was needed at home.

The major purpose for this trip to Dave's brother Bill's place in Atherley was to pick up the pump and plumbing fixtures and some Eaton's Christmas catalogue items that had arrived from Toronto. But this excursion had another, and for Becca, very important purpose. They were also going to get Becca's Christmas present: a filly. Becca knew about her gift horse, but she had never seen it and the anticipation was an itch that she could hardly bear. Bill had been keeping the young horse at his place. He had planned to bring her over himself on Christmas Eve, but last night's storm had ruined that idea. The roads were impassable. The big Ford truck Bill used to transport stock and supplies would never make it through on the drifted and still unplowed roads. But thanks to "Mother Bell" a new plan had been hatched.

David and Paul would now take the horse drawn sleigh to Bill's, pick up the goods and lead the filly, tethered behind, back to the farm. It was only an eight mile run along the back concessions and even if they stopped along the way to give the horses a rest and chat with neighbours, they would be back in good time for that night's community supper and Christmas Eve service at the Udney United Church. The cloudless blue sky was beautiful, but the bright sun belied the chill in the air and Mary pulled her sweater more tightly around her.

"Becca, come and take this parcel to your father."

Becca ran to her, and was about to state again her case for inclusion, but Mary held up her hand.

"Before you start, the answer is no! I need your help around here. And besides, you need to prepare a stall for your filly. Bring Shep away too, so the men can get going."

Becca reluctantly ceased her entreaties, delivered the package to the sleigh, called Shep, and the two of them joined her on the back porch.

"Have a safe trip and keep an eye on the weather. Remember you need to be back in time to clean up for the church supper and Christmas Eve service, so don't spend too much time at 'The Arms' gabbing with Bill. Telephone when you're leaving Atherley so we know you are on your way."

David nodded, snapped the long reins and called "hi up!" Atlas and Hercules pricked their ears, leaned into their collars and pulled away.

Mary and Becca waved goodbye as their men drove out of sight. Shep bounded from the porch to follow the team down the lane as far as the road.

†

Mary shivered and went back inside. Becca followed as far as the door mat in the kitchen.

"Mom, have you seen Annie this morning?"

Annie was Becca's special project. When Annie was just a few days old her mother, one of the ubiquitous barn cats, had been stepped on by a milk cow, leaving her newborn kitten an orphan; hence her name.

Becca had discovered the kitten alone and helpless and decided to raise her. Into the house Annie came and through a combination of a warm basket by the wood stove, cow's milk and Becca's loving attention, she survived. Annie was now a house cat who earned her keep as a mouser.

"No," Mary replied. "Did you feed her this morning?"

"Yes, but her food is still in the bowl on the porch and she didn't come to the barn for her treat when Paul and I were milking this morning."

"Well, she's almost due and cats like to find their own secret place to have their kittens. Did you look in the hayloft?"

"Yes, but there is no sign of her. I'm a little worried. This is her first litter."

"She'll be fine; cats have been having kittens without human help for a long time. Have you finished your chores?"

"All done except for mucking out 'the boys'' stalls."

"Good, go and finish that and let Ranger into the corral for a while. Then come back. I can use your help with the pies." With three headed to the church supper that night, and two for their Christmas dinner the next day, Mary could use a baker's helper.

Becca left for the barn. It was still sunny out, but a breeze had sprung up out of the west, making the air feel colder than it really was. Shep, back from his escort duties, met her at his dog house near the woodpile. He was a working dog who only used his house for shelter during inclement weather, but when winter arrived he too was accorded a warm spot by the stove. Becca opened the small door to the barn and she and Shep entered. She loved the smell of the barn in early winter. The scent of still fresh second cut hay and straw, blended with that of leather harness oiled and hung for ready use, the odour of cows and horses and the taint of manure, enveloped her and made her feel welcome. She flicked the light switch and the row of bare bulbs hanging from the centre beam of the barn began to glow. There were very few and they weren't very bright but it was so much better than having to light the lanterns. Those still hung on each pillar, ready for emergency use, which had been often so far this December.

It seemed that every time there was a storm a line would go down somewhere and they would lose service. She enjoyed working in the barn, milking, feeding the animals and collecting eggs from the chicken enclosure at the far end. Mucking out the stalls was her least favourite chore but it had to be done. Paul and Dad usually did it, but while they were on the road she would clean Atlas' and Hercules' stalls and replace the bedding. And after she put Ranger in the paddock, she might as well do his stall too. Last but not least she would prepare the empty stall beside Ranger to receive her Christmas present. Now that she would have her own horse, moving manure and laying fresh bedding would become a daily chore for her too. Getting indoor plumbing and having a real toilet and bathtub for the family was a great gift, but finally having her own horse was simply wonderful.

She greeted Ranger with kind words and a muzzle rub. The pure white four year old gelding was Paul's horse and no one else rode him. Paul had gotten him two years ago as his public school graduation gift from their parents. Her mother didn't ride and to avoid using the tractor and fuel unnecessarily, if she or Dad needed to visit the back forty or the bush lot, they walked or rode one of "the boys" bareback.

She took Ranger's worn bridle from its hook and fitted it, then led Ranger from the stall, thinking about her Christmas gift for Paul. She had saved some of her egg money to get him a new bridle. It was a jet black, with bright silver fasteners. It would gleam and sparkle in the July sun when Paul rode Ranger in the Orange parade next summer. She couldn't wait to see his face when he unwrapped it on Christmas morning. She opened the big Dutch door to the paddock and released Ranger into the drift-filled yard. He pranced about shaking clinging clumps of snow from his hooves and tossing his head, as much as to say, what's this stuff? He trotted about for a while and then stood, coat quivering, surveying the strange new landscape outside the rails. He looked like Pegasus, as vaporous clouds from his warm body and breath formed pseudo wings around him. Becca left the upper half of the door open so Ranger could watch her if he chose.

As she walked back to get the pitchfork, shovel and wheel barrow she called again for Annie. "Here kitty, kitty! Milk for the kitty!"

A number of barn cats appeared, meowing in the loft above her, but there was no sign of Annie.

Annie usually came to the barn only at milking time to get a treat, and otherwise seldom wandered. She took her role as a house cat seriously. Except of course when she was "courting." One of those outings had resulted in her current condition and she was due to litter any day now. Becca was worried about her. No matter, chores came first. She rolled the wheelbarrow up to Hercules' stall and started to work.

†

Although a foot deep on the level, the crisp new snow offered little resistance to the sleigh's runners and when the horses pulled away, it slid smoothly into motion. Dave smiled as he surveyed the scene from the driver's seat.

It was a beautiful winter morning. What more could a man ask for—a wonderful family, a good farm to support them and a promising future? He glanced at Paul beside him and noted joy there too, in his son's expression. Even the horses were energized. High-stepping their way toward the road their feathered hooves kicked up billows of snow that settled on their burnished coats and sparkled like silver sequins in the sunlight. His "boys" hadn't had a workout since they were forced to help draw in the second cutting of hay in September. Atlas and Hercules were heavy horses bred to farm work and before Dave had purchased a used tractor from his brother Bill, they had done all of the work on the Stone farm.

They drew the plough and seeder in the spring and in summer they pulled the binder and wagons to cut and bring in the hay. They hauled logs from the woodlot and if Dave needed to travel to the back forty to track down cattle, he often rode one of his "boys." In good weather they drew the family to church by wagon and in the winter they loved to haul the sleigh or cutter on local trips, and sometimes as far as Brechin and Atherley. They had proven invaluable over the last few years. Last fall when the tractor broke down, they had saved the day during the harvest. And to top it off they won the heavy horse pull at the Brechin Fall Fair.

"Dad, can I drive?" asked Paul.

Dave grinned and handed him the reins. "Alright, but pay attention and watch them carefully today. They are as excited as we are about this run. It's a sixteen mile round trip to your Uncle Bill's place and we'll have lots of weight coming back, so keep the pace slow and steady. At this rate we should reach there by noon. We can load up, have lunch with him at 'The Arms' and be back on the road by around two. That should leave us plenty of time to get back home, settle Becca's filly into her new home, unload and clean up for the trip to the church supper."

Paul nodded, "Right Dad."

He was a fine boy. Though just fifteen he had carried a man's workload on the farm since his grandparents died. Daily, both before and after attending school at the Orillia District Collegiate, he was responsible for much of the care of the livestock, and of course his own horse Ranger always got special attention.

As they neared the county road Dave noted the snowplow had not yet been by. He was not surprised. Highway #12 got first attention, followed by the county roads, and then the concessions and lines. It was just as well. The snow cushioned the fall of the horses' hooves and the sleigh's runners slid easily. Dave planned to run the back roads all the way to his brother's. It would take a little longer, but they shouldn't encounter any motor vehicles that might crowd or spook the horses. Besides this was the first run this year in the sleigh. He had already noted some wobbling in the right front runner and some other creaks and groans that needed attention. He hadn't had time to make a trial run and fix any problems, but if they were forced to make running repairs, they could stop at one of the farms along the way.

As they exited the driveway, Paul skillfully turned the team on to the county road. Dave glanced to the west. Although the sky overhead was clear, far in the distance he could see a cloud mass building over Georgian Bay. This was the season for snow squalls and streamers off the bay and they had been particularly heavy this year. Last night's storm was a good example of their unpredictability.

Winter had come late to Central Ontario and Georgian Bay had not yet frozen over. Now that the colder temperatures had arrived, the water evaporating from the bay formed massive snow clouds which drifted south and east, dropping their burden into the snowbelt areas of Barrie and Orillia. Last night's storm was supposed to have struck south and west of Orillia, nearer Barrie, but Mother Nature changed her mind. The wind shifted and a fast moving streamer struck farther to the north and east, bringing blizzard conditions to the Orillia and Brechin area instead.

The forecast called for more of the same. But on the radio this morning the weatherman had predicted that today Barrie would get the brunt, while Orillia and district would escape the worst; so he had decided to make the trip to Bill's. Well, they were on the road now and he really did want to have Becca's filly waiting in a stall, where she could groom her on Christmas morning. So he leaned back, put his feet up on the foot rail and began to enjoy the ride.

When Becca returned to the house she hung her outdoor clothes on the hooks and left her boots in the porch room before entering the kitchen. The warmth and riot of delicious aromas that greeted her here were even more to her liking. Her mother had finished rolling out the dough for the pie crust and preparing the filling for the five apple pies. She had just removed the bread from the oven and it sat steaming on the shelf at the back of the stove. Two large copper kettles filled with water were heating on the top of the wood stove. Becca took one and poured a little hot water into the wash bowl and cooled it with a dipper of water from the pail. She washed up and declared herself ready to help.

After her mother finished pressing the dough into each pie plate, Becca would spoon the spicy chunks of her mother's special apple filling into the shells. Once the pies were topped and placed in the oven to bake, she and Mum would haul out the galvanized tub and put it near the stove. Becca would partially fill it from the buckets of well water by the stove and then warm it with hot water from the copper kettles. She and Mum would bathe and dress for church while the men were absent.

Dave made the last few turns to tighten the nut on the replacement bolt. It was not the right size but he felt it would hold for the trip home.

It was certainly better than the bailing wire they had borrowed at the Robinson farm, and rigged to hold the runner's strut in place until they reached Bill's. The whole process had delayed them. It was already well past 3:00 pm and they hadn't loaded the sleigh yet. They still had time to get home by dark but they would have to be quick about it. Between the three of them they hoisted the wooden crates containing the bathtub, toilet and pump into the back of the sleigh, and fitted the copper piping and the brown paper wrapped parcels from Eaton's in as best they could. It was an awkward load.

Dave took the reins while Paul finished tying the filly's lead rope to the hitch on the back of the sleigh. She was a beautiful chestnut brown with a distinct white blaze on her forehead. The little chestnut was none to happy about leaving the warmth of the barn. She pranced and pulled against the lead rope and Bill had to hold her while Paul tied the knot.

Bill pointed to the west at the mass of dark cloud rolling in across Lake Couchiching. Just like last night the wind had shifted and it looked as if they were going to get hit with another streamer squall.

"You're sure you won't stay the night Dave? It could get pretty bad out there. You could leave early in the morning and be home in time for a late Christmas breakfast. You can telephone Mary from here and let her know about the change in plan."

Dave had considered doing just that but he was reluctant to leave his women alone on Christmas Eve, especially if a storm did strike.

"No Bill, Mary and Becca will be expecting us and I'll get the devil from them if they miss the church supper and Christmas Eve service. Even if it does blow and snow a bit we're only an hour or so away, at a good clip, and 'the boys' can find their way home blindfolded. But you can call them and let them know we are on our way. Mary will be fretting about getting her pies to the supper and Becca will be anxious about her filly."

Paul climbed up to join him on the seat. Dave called "hi up," snapped the reins and Atlas and Hercules pulled away. The sky had already begun to darken as the clouds to the west blocked out the soon to be setting sun; the first wind driven flakes of snow were starting to fall.

†

Mary was sitting at the kitchen table enjoying a cup of tea when the telephone rang. Two long one short; that was their ring. She lifted the receiver, placed it to her ear and spoke into the funnel shaped mouth piece on the telephone box.

"Hello."

"Oh, hi Bill. How long ago did Dave and Paul leave, we were expecting them about now?"

"Just a few minutes ago? Don't tell me you two got to jawing at 'The Arms.'"

"Oh, I see."

"It's blowing up quite a bit here, what's the weather like over your way?"

The electric lights in the kitchen flickered, as if in response to her question.

"Coming in from the northwest, eh, just like last night? Well, I'm sure Dave will have sense enough to turn back and..."

The lights flickered again and then went out. The telephone line went dead. The storm had struck and her men were caught out on the road.

†

Dave had badly misjudged the weather. The conditions had deteriorated rapidly into a blizzard. But he had confidence in his team. The "boys" were pulling away smartly. They too wanted to get home and out of the bitter wind and driving snow. He and Paul tied their scarves around their heads to protect their face and ears and spread the blanket from the seat box across their legs. It was getting colder, but home was just a few miles away. They would make it.

Dave reckoned they were near Uptergrove when disaster struck. The jury-rigged bolt on the right front runner let go. The sleigh slewed to the right and headed for the side of the road. It lurched sideways, went over the edge, and tipped. He was thrown violently against Paul and they both were tossed from their perch on the driver's seat into the snow-filled ditch. The crates holding their fixtures lay scattered around them and some of the other parcels and pieces of pipe lay nearby.

Fortunately the sleigh had not tipped further, all the way over on to them. It had been held by the horses, who were now panicking, prancing and pulling against the dead weight.

Dave scrambled to his feet, clawed his way up the embankment and hurried to them.

"Whoa, easy boys, easy." The horses settled.

Paul appeared by his side. He was holding a hand to his forehead and seemed a little disoriented.

"Are you all right son?" Dave asked.

Paul nodded, "I guess so. Something hit me in the head when we landed in the ditch. I think it was the toilet."

"Let's have a look."

Paul took his hand away. It was past dusk, almost dark now, but there was enough light for Dave to examine the injury. He didn't like what he saw. Paul had a large cut on his forehead, just above his left eye. It didn't seem too deep and wasn't bleeding very much, but the surrounding area was already beginning to swell. He must have taken more than a glancing a blow. Indeed, he might even have a concussion. That eye would soon be swollen shut.

"It doesn't look too bad," he told Paul, "but you had better get some ice on it to keep the swelling down."

"Sure... ok Dad." He reached down, scooped up a handful of snow and applied it to the wound. He smiled wryly. "I'll hold the horses while you check out the damage."

Dave went around the rear of the sleigh and surveyed the scene. The cause of the crash, the front runner, had come completely off the strut and was twisted sideways. The sleigh had settled into the roadside snow bank and seemed no longer in danger of tipping completely over. They could probably use the horses to pull the sleigh upright but even if they did he doubted he could re-attach the runner in the dark, during a blizzard. They would travel no further in it tonight. He returned to the front to discuss their options with Paul.

Paul had a firm hold on the horses, but he looked pale and had begun shivering. Given his son's condition Dave decided not to suggest unhitching the horses and riding them home. Even if they rode double he was afraid that if Paul was concussed and went into shock, they would be in worse straits. They had best seek shelter nearby, or create their own refuge right here and sit out the storm.

He was about to broach the idea when Paul spoke. "How's the filly Dad? She was on a long lead so she shouldn't have had a problem."

Dave's heart skipped a beat. The filly! In all the confusion he had forgotten about her! He left Paul's question unanswered and hurried to the back of the sleigh. The little chestnut was gone. The metal hitch on the rear of the sleigh was missing. The filly's lead rope had been tied to it. It could have pulled off during the accident or even sooner. Dave had no way of knowing. Becca's horse was lost and alone in the storm.

†

Mary hung up the telephone ear piece and called to Rebecca, who was drying her hair by the stove.

"Becca, go and get a lamp from the sitting room. We're back on coal oil until the power lines get fixed and I expect that won't be tonight."

She took a match from the holder on the wall beside the stove, struck it, lifted the glass and lit the lamp that still hung from the beam over the sink. Now at least they had light.

Becca returned with the lamp and Mary lit it too and placed it in the centre of the kitchen table.

"Leave your hair, Becca. I don't think we will be going out to supper and church tonight. This storm seems worse than the one last night. Get another cup and join me for tea. I've got something to tell you."

Becca took the news about her Dad and Paul quietly, but inside her heart was beating wildly and her mind was racing. What should they do? Should she take Ranger and Shep and go looking? It was a blizzard out there and they must be having trouble. Her mother answered her unspoken question.

"I know what you want to do. So do I, but don't even think it. Our job is to look after things here and be ready for them when they do get home. While I light a lantern, go and put this lamp in the upstairs bedroom window, where it can be seen from the road. Then we'll go down to the barn. The cows need to be milked and the stock fed, watered and bedded down for the night. Let's get to it. By the time we finish I am sure the men will be home, with a tale to tell."

Becca left with the lamp. Mary began to prepare the lantern for the trip to the barn, wishing all the while that she felt as confident as she sounded about the fate of her men.

Mary and Becca finished their chores quickly. Becca called again for Annie, but she did not appear and reluctantly they doused the last barn lantern and stepped out into the night. The wind was even stronger now and driving the snow in a solid curtain of white across the yard. They could see barely ten steps ahead, but with Becca holding the lantern and Shep leading the way they made their way back toward the house. When they stopped at the woodpile to gather some extra logs for the stove, they could hardly see the back porch. Shep was standing by his dog house barking and their hopes rose, but it wasn't in response to anyone approaching. They reached the back door and Becca called him inside.

Mary shook out her scarf in the porch and stepped into the kitchen. "Let's have a bite to eat. You go and light the lamps and the stove in the sitting room while I get something ready."

The sitting room was just off the combined kitchen and dining area. It was where they gathered each night to do schoolwork, read and listen to the radio. Becca took a handful of matches and went in. There were two large couches and three big comfy chairs grouped facing the Quebec heater, which helped the McClary warm the house on particularly cold nights. Their precious piano sat in one corner and the Christmas tree stood proudly in the other. She lighted two of the table lamps and then kindled and lit the stove. As she turned to leave, something glinted and caught her eye. It was the star that topped their tree. The tree was very simply decorated with ornaments passed down through the family for years; there were no lights. But she herself had cut cardboard in the shape of the Christmas Star and covered it with foil saved from used tea containers. Struck by light from the flickering lamps, it came to life and gleamed atop the tree. Her mother entered carrying their snack on a tray, placed it on the low table by the chairs and put her arm around her.

"Well there is not much under that tree, yet," she said. And that was so. Only three packages lay beneath. One contained an assortment of preserves for her brother-in-law Bill, one wrapped in a discarded sugar bag was Becca's gift for Paul. The remaining gift was hidden in an empty grain bag, which really didn't disguise it. It was a saddle. Paul had refurbished his old one and was giving it to his sister. When the filly was ready to ride next summer, she would need it. They would sleep here on the couches tonight and pray, hope and wait for the safe arrival of their men. That would be their best Christmas gift.

It was now pitch black and the storm had worsened. Dave had considered his options and decided to seek shelter off the road. Paul was insisting that the loss of the filly was his fault and he wanted to go looking for her. That was out of the question and after his father's initial refusal to allow it, Paul knew not to argue. Just before the storm closed in, Dave had seen a large stand of spruce trees off to the right. He walked back a bit farther behind the sleigh and spotted what looked like a level area running across the ditch toward the fence. He called Paul to him.

"Your eyes are better than mine. Is that a driveway?"

Paul walked gingerly across what felt like solid ground, heading toward the fence. As he got closer the snow swirled aside enough for him to see that there was a gate, and it was open! He hurried back to the sleigh.

"It is a driveway Dad, and the gate is open."

Dave made his decision. "Well, there must be something at the end of it. Unhitch the horses, we're going for a walk."

They started up the drive, each leading a horse. The snow was not too deep but in the "white-out" conditions the visibility was nil. Paul was in the lead with Atlas. Suddenly he called out, "Dad, did you see that?"

"See what son?"

"A bright light right above those trees ahead. It looked like a star. I just caught a glimpse of it when the wind dropped."

Dave wondered if the blow to the head was causing Paul to see things.

"No son, I didn't, but if you did let's head for it."

They continued to plod forward into the storm, and then Paul called out once more. "There it is again! Here, hold Atlas."

He left the horse and before Dave could stop him, Paul ran ahead, disappearing into the blizzard.

The minutes that passed seemed like hours. Dave stood holding the horses, waiting for his son's return. Instead he heard him call.

"Dad, bring up the horses!"

Dave began leading the horses up the road, which started to curve slightly, and when he rounded the last stand of trees he too saw the light. It wasn't a star.

It was a cross; a holy cross atop a tall structure. He now knew where they were. They had come up the rear driveway of the St. Columbkille Catholic Church!

Suddenly the light flickered and went out.

"Dad, it's a Catholic Church and we're Orangemen. What should we do?"

Dave considered his reply carefully. Dislike, even hatred between Protestants and Catholics ran deep in this part of Ontario and he was loathe to seek assistance.

But his son was hurt and they were caught in a blizzard. He would ask for help.

"Come on son, let's knock on their door."

Father O'Malley was in the Sacristy when he heard the pounding at the back door. Who could that be, he wondered. The word had gone out on the party lines that tonight's Mass had been cancelled due to the storm. He was sure most had gotten the message before the lines went dead and the electric power was cut. Maybe someone hadn't. But why the back door? The front door was always open. He picked up the coal oil lamp from his desk and headed down the rear stairs to greet his mysterious Christmas Eve visitor. The knocking continued.

"I'm coming, I'm coming. Hold your horses!"

And they were, literally. He opened the door and was confronted by two men holding huge horses. "What in Heaven's name?"

The shorter one had one eye swollen shut and stood silent. The taller removed his hat and spoke.

"Excuse us for disturbing you, Father. We've had an accident on the road and my son has been hurt. We are seeking shelter."

"Yes, yes, of course." He leaned forward to push the door open, then paused. "But you don't attend this church. To what Parish do you belong? Brechin? or perhaps Orillia?"

"We attend the United Church in Udney," said Dave firmly.

"I see." He straightened up in the doorway. "Orangemen too, no doubt? Seeking refuge in a Catholic Church? What's your name son?"

Paul spoke up clearly. "Paul Stone, sir. And what's yours?"

The priest smiled. "Ah, a right proper lad you are. I'm Father O'Malley."

His gaze shifted toward Dave.

"Then you must be David Stone, and these are Atlas and Hercules."

"Your answer, Father?" said Dave.

"Well," said Father O'Malley, "it may have been a night much like this when two weary travelers sought shelter, so that their child might be born. And I believe that, despite our differences, we will both be celebrating that child's birth tomorrow. I think He would welcome you. So should I. There is a lean-to barn to your left, where my parishioners who still come by cutter stable their horses. Now that our Mass has been cancelled no one will be using it. You can bed them down there. Wait here for a moment while I get a lantern."

Father O'Malley returned momentarily and handed Dave a lantern.

"Mr. Stone, you take care of the horses and while you're doing that I'll have a look at the lad's injury."

Paul looked to his father for direction.

"Thank you Father," said Dave. "Please do."

Dave nodded to Paul and then led the team toward the stable.

"Follow me lad," said Father O'Malley.

Paul followed the priest inside and up the stairs to the Sacristy. Father O'Malley pointed to a chair and invited him to sit. He went to the sideboard and filled a small golden bowl with water from a pitcher, wetted a cloth and brought them both to the table.

"Let's have a look son."

Paul tilted his head and pushed the hair off his forehead to enable Father O'Malley to swab the cut.

"What hit you?"

Paul hesitated. "I think a toilet," he said, and hastily explained the purpose of their trip.

"I see," said the priest. "Well I wouldn't be telling that to your friends me lad. Perhaps you could just say a crate?"

Paul smiled, and spoke up.

"Father, how did you know our name? Do you have spies?"

"No, my son. I saw your magnificent horses pull at the Brechin Fair last fall. I wasn't sure at first but when you gave your name, I put two and two together. The cut doesn't look too bad. It could take a stitch or two but it's too late now for that. But I am going to disinfect it. You'll have a small scar, but I doubt the girls will notice it when you ride as King Billy on July 12th next year. That's a beautiful horse you have."

Paul was taken aback once more.

"How do you know about that? It's an Orange parade."

"Of course it is my son, but everybody likes a parade, so I make a point of attending. Now hold still while I do this."

The priest poured some liquid from a small golden pitcher into the bowl, dipped the cloth and proceeded to cleanse the wound. It stung, but Paul didn't flinch.

"What is that Father?"

"Just a little sacramental wine; some alcohol to kill the germs."

While the priest worked Paul spoke again.

"Father, if your electricity went off hours ago how did the cross stay lighted. We might not have found you if I hadn't seen it. In the storm it looked like a star... the Christmas star... and it led us here."

"A star you say; and on Christmas Eve. Well my boy, that is a mystery, because that cross hasn't been lit for a month now; ever since the big storm in November. I had hoped to have it repaired for Christmas Eve Mass, but the parts haven't come from Toronto yet."

"Then how... ?"

"My son, our Lord works in mysterious ways, and what better time than tonight for Him to do so?"

Dave entered the room.

"The horses are settled in. What about Paul, Father?"

"Well, I've examined and cleaned the wound; and even though he says he was seeing stars I think he'll be fine. Hard-headed, like most Orangemen I dare say."

Dave smiled in spite of himself.

"Thank you Father. We'll be going now. I have fixed up a bed for us in the stable and we'll sleep there tonight."

"Well, you can sleep there if you choose, Mr. Stone, but I recommend that Paul sleep indoors. He needs to stay warm. He can use that couch."

Paul was about to protest when his Father stopped him.

"Paul, you will do what the Father says."

"And you Mr. Stone should stay here with him. He took a nasty blow to the head and could have a concussion. You should wake him every couple of hours or so to be sure he is alright. You can doze in that chair if you like."

Dave reluctantly accepted the father's advice. "If you think that is best Father, I will."

"Good. Now sit. You must be hungry and thirsty. I brought a plate of sandwiches over from the rectory earlier, but your arrival interrupted my meal. There is enough for you to share and water in the pitcher on the sideboard."

"What about you?"

Father O'Malley patted his rather ample belly. "I'll survive until I get back to the rectory."

He gathered up the sandwich plate, three silver chalices and joined his guests at the table. He filled a cup with water for Paul and his own goblet from the wine pitcher.

"To ward off the chill," he advised. "Will you join me Mr. Stone?"

Dave hesitated, then nodded his head in reply. Sharing sacramental wine with a priest in a Catholic church on Christmas Eve, was not something he had ever envisioned doing; but in for a penny in for a pound. He proffered his cup. Paul reached for a sandwich.

"Paul, remember your manners." Paul bowed his head.

" God Bless this food to our use and Father O'Malley for helping us tonight. Amen."

"Amen," repeated the father. "Now tell me more about those magnificent horses of yours. How old are they?"

Mary lay still awake. Becca had finally dozed off but sleep had eluded her. The wind was still howling and if anything the storm seemed to be growing in intensity. Their tree top star twinkled with the light from the single lamp they had left burning. She knew deep down that Dave and Paul were probably fine but she could not help worrying. That star had led other travelers to refuge many years ago and perhaps it was watching over her family tonight. She hoped so. She focused on it, said a silent prayer and closed her eyes to sleep.

†

Dave gently shook Paul awake.

"Up you get son, it's time to go."

Paul sat up and rubbed the sleep from his eyes. "Ooow…my head. What time is it?"

"Time we were on the road. Wait'll you see how we are getting home."

Paul pulled on his boots, grabbed his coat and hat and donned them as he followed his father down the stairs to the rear door. He was greeted by a surprising if not amazing sight. Atlas and Hercules stood ready, in harness to a large cutter. It was black and had an ornate gold cross painted on its side. The words St. Columbkille Church, also in gold, were painted along the length of the sleigh's body. Father O'Malley stood with the horses, stroking their muzzles and talking to them.

"Dad, we can't…"

Dave forestalled him. "Father O'Malley offered and I have accepted, graciously. We can reload the small items and be home in time for a late Christmas breakfast with the women. Are you up for it?"

"You bet!" Paul ran to the horses.

"Top o' the mornin' to you lad. Did you sleep well?"

"Yes Father, thank you."

"How's your head?"

"Better. I still have a headache, but I'll survive."

"Ah, that you will lad, just as I suspected, hard-headed."

Dave climbed aboard and Paul joined him.

"Thank you Father O'Malley for your kindness, both last night and this morning. I'll return your cutter as soon as I can."

"I expect you will. I wish I was riding with you. I would like to see how it feels to handle a team like yours. But duty calls me here. And you lad, next year on the 12th, when you're ridin' that fine horse of yours in the parade, look for me and wave mind you! Merry Christmas to you both and your family."

"Merry Christmas Father!"

Dave flicked the reins and called "hi up!" They were on their way home for Christmas.

†

Mary was up with the sun. The men had not returned. She rekindled the stove, put the kettle on and tried the radio. No response. The power was still off. She woke Becca.

"Merry Christmas dear!"

"Are they home?"

"No, and if they stayed somewhere for the night I wouldn't be expecting them yet. Let's have some tea and toast, then we can do the milking and collect the eggs. By the time we finish they might be home and we can have breakfast together."

It was another beautiful winter morning, sunny but cold. The sky was crystal blue and there wasn't a hint of snow in the air. Becca noted on the walk to the barn that the snow wasn't much deeper, but the drifts had been moved around and spread everywhere. The wood pile was almost covered and Shep's house was buried to the roof line. She had to clear away snow in order to open the small barn door. Everything was just as she had left it. Although bright sunlight was filtering in through the cracks and spaces in the barn-board, they still needed to light some lanterns. They had finished the milking, feeding and watering and were just preparing to collect the eggs when they heard Shep barking. Becca dropped her basket and ran. She burst out of the barn door.

It was them! They were home and safe!

But what were they driving? She got to the cutter just as her father was descending and jumped into his arms. They both started talking at once and Shep's barks added to the confusion. Mary hurried up and hugged her son, then she held him at arm's length.

"What happened to you?" she exclaimed. "You're hurt!"

Dave spoke up. "He'll be fine. Father O'Malley said so."

"Who?"

Shep bounded in between them, put his paws on Paul's chest and barked even louder!

Everyone started talking at once.

"Enough!" said Dave. "Paul you take the horses to the barn. Feed them and bed them down. The rest of us will go in to the kitchen and I'll begin telling our tale, while we get breakfast started. You can fill in the gaps when you return. Let's go."

They gathered at the kitchen table. The first order of business was to tell Becca about the loss of her horse. That was why he'd sent Paul to the barn. Paul had spent much of the trip home lamenting the filly's loss and blaming himself for not securing her properly. Dave assured Paul that if anyone was at fault it was himself, but Paul was still upset. Dave didn't waste any time.

"Becca, I have bad news. On our way home our sleigh went in the ditch. Your filly was lost in the storm. I don't know how, where, or even when. Your brother was hurt and we were caught in the blizzard. We couldn't look for her. I'm sorry."

Becca took the news stoically, but her eyes began to well. "Did you look this morning?"

"Yes we did, on the way home, but there was no sign of her and we saw no tracks. I am afraid she's gone dear. Maybe she'll turn up at a farm nearby," he placed his big hand over her smaller one on the table, "and if not, we'll be able to afford another horse soon."

Paul entered. "I'm sorry Becca, I should have tied her tighter."

Becca held her voice steady. "Dad said it was no one's fault. I can wait a little longer. Let's hear the whole story. What happened to your head?"

Dave interrupted, "Let's start at the beginning."

And he and Paul took turns telling their tale and answering all of the questions about their Christmas Eve adventure. During the telling the telephone rang. One long continuous ring.

"That's the 'all pick up' signal," said Paul. His mother lifted the ear piece, listened and then hung up.

"Well, as you can hear, the phones are working and they expect to have the electricity back on soon. Last night's church service has been rescheduled to late this afternoon and the church supper will follow at the hall. They say the main roads will be cleared by then and the whole community can celebrate Christmas together."

It was welcome news! By the time they finished eating, talking about last night's storm, planning to retrieve their sleigh from St. Columbkille's and for their trip to church, everyone was feeling better.

Paul piped up, "Heh, it's Christmas. Let's open our presents!"

Becca's eyes closed and she ducked her head for a moment. Then she looked up and smiled. "Let's go. Wait until you see what I got you."

It didn't take them long to open the few parcels under the tree. Paul was surprised and delighted by the bridle. Becca of course knew what his gift to her was, but she removed the saddle from its bag anyway and noted that the polishing and repairs Paul had done had made it look almost as good as new.

"Thanks Paul," she said. "Maybe I will be able to use it next year."

"Why not this year?" he replied. "You can ride Ranger, whenever you want."

Becca smiled. "Thanks Paul, but he's your horse. I can wait."

Shep started barking again and Paul ran to the window.

"It's Uncle Bill. He's driving his big truck. Everyone headed for the drive-yard grabbing their coats and boots on the way. They found Bill standing, staring at the cutter.

"I see you got home alright. Where in the devil did you get that?"

"Merry Christmas to you too," said Dave. "We got caught in the storm and spent the night on the road. I'll tell you all about it later." There were hugs and Christmas greetings all round and then quiet.

"What are you doing here?" asked Dave.

"When you left my place you forgot something. Becca come and help me."

Becca joined Bill at the back of the truck. He opened the double doors wide. There stood Becca's filly.

Becca jumped into the truck and threw her arms around the chestnut's neck.

"Oh, Uncle Bill, she's alive! You saved her!"

"Well, not really," Bill replied. "She showed up at my barn about fifteen minutes after your Dad left. I was battening down for the storm when she came in dragging her tether rope with the sleigh hitch still attached. Paul, help me with the ramp."

Becca untied her Christmas gift and led her down to the ground. She was beautiful. Her rich brown coat shone in the late afternoon sun and the silver blaze on her forehead stood out proudly.

What are you going to call her Becca?" asked her mother.

Becca smiled. "I thought of lots of names before, but now that I've seen her. Look at the shape of her blaze." She stroked it. "It's a star. Her name is Star. Becca's Star."

"Take Star to the barn and put her in her stall Becca. You can stay with her a while and get her settled but then come up and get ready for church. Will you join us for the service and supper Bill?"

"Did you bake pies Mary?" She nodded. "Then I wouldn't miss it. But I need to go in and get cleaned up. Dave, I'll need to borrow a pullover."

By the time they had retold their tale and prepared for church it was dusk. Paul and Dave hitched Atlas and Hercules to the cutter and they were ready to leave. As Mary was gathering her pies Dave stopped her.

"Leave one here, dear. Paul and I have to return the cutter tomorrow. I know someone who will appreciate your cooking."

Mary smiled and left a pie.

As they were boarding the sleigh Bill couldn't contain himself. "Riding in style Dave. I can't wait to hear you explain to the fellas how you came to be driving a 'papist' cutter to church on Christmas Day. And Paul ,what was it that gave you that shiner, a toil..."

"It was a crate!" interrupted Paul.

Shep started barking as the sleigh started to move. The yard was lit brightly by the big farm safety light and they could see him standing by the snow-covered entrance to his dog house, snuffling in the drift.

"What is wrong with that dog today?" said Mary.

"Maybe he just wants to get inside. Hold on Dad." Paul jumped down beside the doghouse and began to move the snow aside with his boot. Then he heard a sound. He pushed aside the door flap and looked in. "Becca! Come here, look."

Becca dropped to her knees. "Mum, Dad, it's Annie. She's got two, no, three kittens. I had better..."

"Leave her be Becca. She's fine for now. You can bring them all in when we get home. Now get aboard you two."

Paul and Becca climbed into the back of the cutter and sat flanking their uncle.

Dave flicked the reins, called "hi up" and they were off.

When his father turned the cutter onto the county road Paul was facing west toward Atherley. Their barn sat directly in the path of his gaze. Although the sky was cloudless there was just a hint of snow mist in the crisp air. He pointed.

"Look there, off in the distance, right over the barn. It's that star again. The one I saw last night."

"I don't see anything," said Bill.

"I saw it," said Becca. "But it's gone now."

"It's still there," said Dave. "Even when we can't see it." He smiled at his wife.

"It was there when others needed it, and when we needed it. It will shine forever in peace and hope, so long as we believe and celebrate the meaning and magic of Christmas."

"Amen," said Mary.

Home For Christmas?

THE HIGH PITCHED VOICES OF THE TWO YOUNG WOMEN in the paddock could be heard clearly from the upstairs bedroom of the Stone family farmhouse. Despite the sobering purpose of her task Mary Stone smiled. She gave the quilt in her hand an extra fold, laid it at the foot of the bed and went to the open window. Even though it was late December the air was fresh rather than frigid. Today marked the third in a row of sunny skies and above freezing temperatures and her girls were taking advantage of it.

The pair could have been sisters, but they were in fact sisters-in-law. Her daughter Rebecca was teaching Susan, her son Paul's wife, to ride. Susan was mounted on Star, Becca's chestnut mare. She was holding the reins and laughing as Becca halter led them on a slow walk around the corral. It was good to hear Susan laugh. It's hard to be happy when your husband is at war, in harm's way, far from home. Susan was the reason Mary was airing and making up Paul's former bedroom. Christmas 1944 was just a week a way and Paul would not be home to celebrate with them.

Paul's last letter contained both good and sad news. He was safe and had almost completed his tour of duty. He had served with distinction; so much so he had already been reassigned as an instructor and would be returning to Canada to take up his post at the air gunnery school in nearby Whitby. He was coming home, but not until the New Year. Susan had remained living in their house on an adjacent farm. But in Paul's absence Mary had insisted that Susan spend Christmas with them.

Becca's Star. Was it really already a decade since that wild winter night, Christmas Eve 1934? Star was to be Becca's Christmas present that year. Winter storms had closed the roads, so her husband Dave and Paul made a special trip by horse-drawn sleigh to pick up the gift filly. But on the return leg they were caught in a blizzard, suffered an accident and were stranded on the road. A mysterious star had guided them to safety at St. Columbkille Catholic Church. Father O'Malley had given them shelter for the night, but the little horse had gone missing in the storm. However, all had ended well. David and Paul made it home safely on Christmas morning and Becca's filly was rescued and aptly named Star. It had been a wondrous Christmas and a good omen.

In the years following, the Stone family had shed the shackles of the Great Depression and begun to prosper. Hard work, good management and some luck contributed to their success. Fortune had smiled when the McIsaac farm next to theirs went up for sale. Bob and Margaret McIsaac had managed their 200 acres well for the past 50 years. But they had no children and had been forced to leave the land and retire to Orillia. Money was still very tight but the McIsaacs took back a small mortgage and the Stones were able to acquire the farm and the milk quota that came with it. They set about combining the farming operations.

With the help of their children Paul and Becca and a hired man, the Stone family farms prospered. Paul had graduated from the Orillia District Collegiate, and was studying agriculture at the University of Guelph. Now a young man he had taken up residence in the former McIsaac house. He and his father worked as partners combining Paul's new knowledge with Dave's experience. They made a good team. Then Hitler invaded Poland and Canada was at war.

The Stone menfolk felt duty bound to report for service and did so over the protests of their women. Thankfully, they encountered a sensible recruiting officer. He rejected Dave's older brother Bill on age and because he was already working in a support industry at Hunter Boats in Orillia. Dave was told outright that his role as a farmer was far more important to the war effort than carrying a rifle. Paul was a different story. He was barely of age and still attending university. A compromise was reached. Paul enlisted in the Air Force Reserve. He would stay in school and train on weekends and in the summer, in preparation for being called up.

Susan was the new addition to the Stone family. Paul had met her at school. When she saw them together at graduation, Mary knew immediately Susan would be the one. After a year of long distance courting, Paul finally asked for her hand. Following a spring wedding in Guelph, Susan went from being a single "city" girl to a married "country" woman. Leaving office work in a Guelph dairy to keep house on a working farm was a challenge. Mary became Susan's mentor and her respect and love for Susan grew as she watched her new daughter-in-law struggle to adapt to country life and being a farm wife. Her son was lucky to have found such a good partner.

Life at war went on. The rationing of sugar and gasoline had to be coped with but otherwise the two Stone farms flourished and did their part to feed the nation and the troops. But the news from overseas was not good. The Battle of Britain was raging and England and her allies stood alone. Then the Japanese attacked Pearl Harbour, the Americans declared war and the whole world was in conflict. Paul was called to active duty.

As a teenager at the Orillia Fall Fair, Paul had gone up in a vintage biplane and fallen in love with flying. He enlisted in the RCAF with hopes of becoming a pilot. But so had others and many had previous experience. The losses suffered by Bomber Command had been devastating; aircrews were badly needed and Paul was transferred to air gunnery school in Whitby. In early July he was given three days leave and orders for overseas duty as a rear gunner in a Lancaster bomber. Mary would never forget the sight of Paul and Susan embracing on the platform at the Udney railway station, and the tears that were shed when Paul swung on board the train to go to war, perhaps never to return.

Well, at least Becca would be here. She too had finished high school and followed her brother to Guelph. She wanted to be a veterinarian. She was in her second year of study and was home for the Christmas holiday.

Enough of this "wool gathering" she thought. It's time to get to work. She called to the girls. "Becca, Susan, put Star in the barn; it's time to get to work. Meet me in the kitchen."

Mary closed the window, surveyed the room and nodded with approval. At least with Susan staying here Paul would be home, if only in "spirit."

†

Airman Paul Stone was fighting to stay alert. It was bitterly cold at 20,000 feet and well below zero in his turret. His heated "Taylor" suit was working overtime. Their Lancaster bomber was five hours out on a seven hour mission and on its way home. A good breakfast and warm bed were just hours away at their base in Kirmington.

His tail turret was the most isolated position in a Lanc. It was basically a pair of machine guns attached to a swivel chair, partially surrounded by a Perspex canopy. The turret actually sat outside of the Lanc's main fuselage, connected only by intercom and an access hatch. The tail gunner was the crew's eyes to the rear, above and below, and their first line of defense since the German fighter aircraft invariably attacked from behind.

This was his final sortie. The Dutch people were starving. Bomber Command had assigned the 166th Squadron to join in a massive Christmas relief effort, dropping food and medical supplies to the people of Holland. It had been a good flight and a positive last mission. The Squadron had flown in formation to the Dutch coast and then separated, each plane heading for their assigned drops over small towns and villages scattered across the Netherlands. They had encountered little anti-aircraft fire over their target and thankfully the German night fighters had not yet appeared. It had been satisfying to hear the bomb aimer cry "Merry Christmas!" rather than "bombs gone," when he dropped their cargo over Amersfoort. Paul patted the left side of his chest and felt reassured. He always carried his personal items with him on a mission. His family pictures were close to his heart in the inside chest pocket of his uniform, and tonight for luck he also carried his reassignment orders. He would be home for Christmas next year for sure.

It was a good night for flying. The moon had set and you could see some stars, although small clouds we scattered both above and below them across the midnight sky. Great cover but also good hiding places for marauding fighters. The steady drone of the Lancaster's four powerful Merlin engines was reassuring, but could lull you to sleep. Paul went through his routine once again. Swiveling his guns at an imaginary attacker he went 'round the clock, sweeping the sky, working the cold and stiffness from his hands and forearms. Then he went back to scanning. He would repeat that routine another 100 times before they landed.

He never saw the fighter that got them. The explosion of cannon shells striking the port side of the Lanc's fuselage was deafening and the plexiglass of Paul's turret shattered around him.

The whole aircraft shuddered in response then yawed to port and began to sideslip, rapidly losing altitude. That probably saved them from the next attacker. Paul saw the second fighter coming in with machine guns blazing, but the sudden loss of altitude caused by his partner's attack must have unsighted the pilot. The tracer fire from his guns was going high. Paul got off a quick burst as their attacker flashed by, but the damage to his turret prevented him from traversing his guns. Then they were gone.

Paul's seat had been twisted violently sideways and if it hadn't been for his safety harness and the fact he was holding on to the gun grips at the time, he might have been thrown out of the aircraft. The intercom was silent as the pilot fought for control and finally leveled off the crippled Lancaster. Paul's ears were still ringing when his helmet intercom crackled to life.

"Pilot to crew, everybody all right? How badly are we hit? I need damage reports."

"Mid-upper sir. He missed me, but number four engine is on fire and the tail, the tail... it's gone sir!"

"Repeat please!"

"Skipper, both vertical stabilizers are gone, well, correct that, the port side one is gone and there is a stub left on the starboard, the..."

"Rear gunner report. Rear gunner! Paul, are you there?"

There was a loud crackling and static over the intercom.

"Roger Skip, I'm still here; barely. Doug's right though, I'm sitting here in what's left of my turret, like a frog on a lily pad."

"Are you hurt?"

"Hit in the left leg. It stings like the devil but I can move it. Probably splinters from the shell that smashed my canopy. I'll live."

"Flight. Larry, what do you think? Can we get this kite home?"

"Maybe sir. We've lost power in number three engine too. We've gotten home on two engines before but, worse case, if we can make the Dutch coast and then some we can ditch in the Channel and hope one of our patrol boats picks us up."

"Navigator. Frank how far are we from the Dutch coast?"

"About 30 miles sir."

"Listen Paul, if I have to put this baby down in the Channel she's going to sink tail first, with you in her. Can you get back into the fuselage?"

"I doubt it Skip, the turret is twisted and the hatch looks jammed."

"Can you bail out?"

"Skipper, I can't abandon..."

"You're not abandoning us, I'm throwing you out! I want you to bail out while we are still over land."

"But...?"

"That is an order Airman Stone. Remember the drill and your training. Get ready, we're still losing altitude. I will cue you when we get a little closer to the coast."

Paul checked his parachute for damage, tightened the straps and waited. His training consisted of two tower jumps and one live jump from altitude.

The drill was simple; pray, pull the ripcord, pray, flex and roll on landing and hope he found help before the Germans found him. His headset crackled in his ears.

"Paul, are you ready?"

"Yes sir."

"Frank says you should come down somewhere near the fishing village of Kamperduin. Good luck son!"

"Thanks Skipper, you guys stay dry and I'll see you back in England. You can stand me to a pint."

Paul unsnapped his safety harness, took a deep breath and tumbled out into the night.

†

Mary stood at the kitchen sink washing up the last of the mixing bowls and spoons. The afternoon's preparations for the church's Christmas Eve supper and their own Christmas dinner had gone very well and done much to rekindle her family's holiday spirit. Her old four burner McClary woodstove was working at capacity and the kitchen was warm and filled with the odour of fresh baking. Susan was flushed with success, having made from scratch her first batch of shortbread cookies. Becca as usual had over-filled the pie shells with preserves and they would probably bubble, but even that was becoming a Stone Christmas tradition. She could hear Dave outback, working at the chopping block, splitting rounds to replenish the wood pile. Becca was drying and putting away dishes. Susan had brewed a pot of tea. She was in the parlour setting out the milk and cookies to go with it. They would ask Dave to join them. Shep's barking drew her eyes to the window. They had a visitor.

Mary looked out to see a battered blue pickup truck pull into the drive-yard. She recognized Charlie Graham's old Ford immediately.

Charlie was Udney's station-master. He was responsible for the Canadian Pacific Railway's freight, passenger and telegraphy services. He had a passenger. Strange, they weren't expecting any packages or visitors by train. Both doors opened and the men stepped out. The passenger was Reverend Campbell their Minister at Udney United. How nice of him to visit. He adjusted his fedora, brushed and straightened his long coat and then removed a paper from his inner coat pocket. It was yellow; that peculiar shade of yellow used for telegrams. Why would he be … she dropped the dish cloth and ran.

Dave was standing with Charlie and Reverend Campbell when Mary arrived. He took her firmly by the shoulders.

"Mary, a telegram has come for Susan."

Mary's voice trembled, "Please come inside. Susan is in the front room."

She led the way. Becca joined the procession. Susan called from the parlour, "Who's here Mum? Are they going to join us for tea? I'll need more cups."

The group entered the room. Susan had lighted the Christmas tree in the corner and was standing by the tea pot that was warming on the Quebec heater. Reverend Campbell spoke softly and extended the paper in his hand.

"Susan this telegram has come for you."

Susan stared at it without saying a word.

Mary stepped to her side, took her arm and invited her to sit on the sofa. The others remained standing. Susan unfolded the paper and read

Dear Mrs. Paul Stone,

We regret to inform you that on December 18, 1944 airman Paul Stone was reported …

The yellow paper fell from Susan's shaking hands and she began to weep.

†

Paul awoke with a splitting headache and a searing pain in his left leg. His right eye was swollen shut. He touched the area gingerly but could find no cut. He struggled to sit up, wincing at the effort. He was in a small room about the size of his horse Ranger's stall in their barn back home. A single candle provided the only light and he was not alone. A man was sitting cross-legged just a few feet away. He looked to be in his fifties or even older. He was not wearing a uniform. His companion was busy examining some items held in his left hand and his right was resting on his thigh inches from the automatic pistol in his lap. Paul checked his uniform pockets; his orders and pictures were missing. The man spoke in a guttural tone. "Sprechen sie Deutsch?"

Paul knew what he meant. "No!"

"Good," replied a pleasant voice with an English accent, "then we can speak English."

"Airman Paul Stone, Royal Canadian Air Force..."

"Relax. You're not a prisoner...yet. A Canuck, *eh*?" he said, with emphasis on the "eh."

"That's right, who are you?"

"I'll ask the questions for now. What's a puck?"

Paul started to think he was in Wonderland, but he didn't feel answering that question would reveal any military secrets.

"It's a round black piece of rubber that we play hockey with."

The man put his pistol aside and handed Paul his papers and photographs.

"Had to be sure. Even German intelligence isn't that good. I'm Charles Goodman, British Intelligence. I trained in your country three years ago. Bloody rough game that hockey."

"You're a spy?"

"We prefer the term intelligence agent."

"Where am I, what day is it?"

"You're inside a haystack on a Dutch farm about three miles from the coast. You've been here for the last two days."

"The last thing I remember was the ground coming up fast and trying to miss a tree. I must have hit it."

"You did, and you're a lucky lad. I was traveling with the 'onderduikers,' the Dutch underground, when your aircraft flew over. One engine was on fire and it was losing altitude. We saw your chute open. We knew the Germans would too and come running. That put us in danger. We got to you first. You were hanging from a branch, out cold, so we just picked you up and carried you here. It sounds like your head is all right. How's the leg?"

Paul looked down and noted the lower left leg of his uniform pants had been slit open and he was bandaged from knee to ankle.

"Well, it hurts like the devil, but if that's the case then it must all still be there."

"It is that," replied Goodman. "I don't think anything's broken, but you have a nasty wound in your calf. There was a big sliver of plastic sticking out. I removed it and applied a makeshift bandage, but I'm sure there are still pieces in there. Do you think you can walk on it?"

There wasn't enough room in their hideout for Paul to stand but he struggled to kneel on his good knee. He pushed himself into a half crouch and flexed his wounded leg. His left knee still worked, but everything below that was on fire.

"I think so, why?"

Goodman checked his watch. "I'm scheduled to leave here tomorrow. If you can walk then you are welcome to join me. We are going fishing first and then catching a fast boat to England."

Paul thought he was back in Wonderland. "What! How are we going to...?"

"Steady lad. We aren't out of it yet and if we are captured the less you know the better. But if things unfold as planned we will be back on British soil before Christmas. My escape was already planned. I wasn't expecting company, but you can't stay here. If you get caught the Dutch family that owns this farm will be shot and if you're lucky you'll end up in a POW camp. Here, eat this and then get some more rest."

He handed Paul a crust of hard black bread about the size of his thumb and a cup of water. "Don't waste even the crumbs. Someone in the den Bruin family went hungry tonight to provide it."

Paul ate in silence, watching Goodman pour over a map, making notes and marking Xs in several places. He didn't bother to ask. He chewed slowly and sipped and savoured the water. He took out his picture of Susan and him, studied it, then carefully returned it to the pocket over his heart and curled up to rest.

†

Susan turned to Mary and buried her face in her shoulder, sobbing; her body racked with grief. Becca reached down, recovered the telegram and read, *"has been reported missing in action."*

"He's missing. Paul is just missing; he could be alright. He will be, I know he will!"

She handed the telegram to her father and joined Susan and her mother on the couch. All three of them cried in relief, in hope, and in fear.

Still standing, Dave read the telegram then walked to the side table near the window. He proffered a decanter of amber liquid.

"Reverend Campbell, Charlie, will you join me?"

Both nodded. Dave poured three glasses and offered a toast.

"To my son, Paul. May he be kept safe and returned to us well and soon," and the men drained their tumblers.

Mary spoke next. Her voice was firm and even.

"David, please go and get the kerosene lamps from the storage closet and bring them here. Reverend Campbell, Charlie, please sit, join us for tea. Susan has made her first shortbread cookies and I am certain they are delicious. Becca will you pour?"

Dave returned with the lamps.

Mary took a matchbox from the shelf on the wall by the Quebec heater and gave it to Susan.

"Susan, many years ago Paul and David were lost in a blizzard on Christmas Eve. Becca and I were home alone and very worried. That night we lit these lamps, placed one on the mantel near the Christmas tree and the other in the upstairs window. They were our beacons of hope and faith, that our men would return safely; and they did on Christmas Day. Now it is your turn."

Susan struck a match and lighted both lamps. Dave moved one to the mantel and left the other with her.

"Let's join in prayer," said Reverend Campbell. "Dear Lord, watch over our lost son, brother, husband and friend, Paul Stone, and in your mercy bring him safely home to us, Amen."

"Thank you, Reverend," said Mary. She turned to her daughter-in-law. "Susan your cookies are still warm from the oven and they smell delightful. Please pass them around. Now Reverend Campbell, about the Church supper on Christmas Eve. I think we've had enough turkeys donated but..."

The conversation turned to happier things as they reviewed plans for the Christmas Eve service and dinner at the church. Susan returned to her seat, politely acknowledging the compliments about her shortbread, but otherwise sat silent. The flames from the oil lamps flickered brightly and were caught and reflected by the polished surface of the silver star atop the Christmas tree. Susan picked up her lamp and politely excused herself. The others watched in quiet sympathy as she left to carry it upstairs to its appointed place.

Paul sat back to back with his British benefactor. They were hidden under a pile of fishing nets on board a Dutch fishing trawler. He was shivering violently and knew he had a fever, but at the moment that was his least concern. The boat's engine was idling and they were preparing to get underway, but there was a loud argument going on very close to their hiding place. He recognized the trawler Captain's voice and knew the other voice was German, but he could not understand their words.

Up until now their escape had gone according to plan. He and Charles had simply hidden in plain sight. Wearing a stocking cap, clothed in an oversized coat to hide his uniform and carrying a hoe, he simply blended in with a group of villagers returning to town from gleaning the local fields. The few Germans soldiers watching paid little attention to a limping man being helped by his companion. Once in the town they were smuggled aboard the fishing boat and hidden, awaiting departure with the evening tide. The crew was just about to cast off when they were hailed from the wharf and the German boarded.

Charles whispered, "The German wants to search the ship. The Captain is telling him he must sail immediately or he'll miss the tide and there will be no fish for anyone, including his commanding officer."

The German's tone changed, a few more words were exchanged and orders were shouted. The crew's boots pounded on the deck as they hurried to cast off, the beat of the engine rose strongly and the boat began to head out to sea.

Once they were clear Paul queried Charles. "Why doesn't the crew just keep on going and escape?"

"Because they are patriots, and brave men. This is the second time they've brought me out. Besides, their families are hostage and the village needs the few fish the Germans will let them keep."

Two hours later the transfer to a British patrol craft went without a hitch. The trawler had it nets deployed and was fishing as usual when a sleek craft arrived at the rendezvous point and slipped in beside her. A young naval Ensign welcomed them aboard, hurried them below deck and then ordered full speed. The engines thundered to life and they were off. The Ensign had been expecting only one passenger, but Charles explained Paul's presence. The naval officer noted the flash on Paul's uniform.

"Welcome aboard Canada. Glad we could help you too. You should feel right at home. This little beauty was built in your country."

He pointed to the large brass manufacturer's plate on the bulkhead.

Paul read the inscription out loud.

"Fairmile Number 24 manufactured by Hunter Boats Orillia Ontario Canada." He smiled. "I don't believe it. It is a smaller world than you know. This boat was built near my home town and I would bet my Uncle Bill had a hand in it."

The Ensign produced a flask and three cups. He poured and raised his in a toast. "To King and Country, the Fairmile and your Uncle Bill."

†

Dave had finished in the barn and was walking toward the house when the large black car pulled into the drive-yard. He knew immediately who the passenger was. The driver exited, hurried around to the passenger door, and offered his hand to the large figure emerging. There was no mistaking the smiling face and familiar voice of Father O'Malley, the patriarch Parish priest at St. Columbkille Catholic Church in Uptergrove.

"Good afternoon to you David!" he boomed, and "Merry Christmas!"

Dave smiled and returned his greeting. Father O'Malley had come to their aid when he and Paul were stranded on that stormy Christmas Eve a decade ago. Despite their religious differences, the good Father had become a family friend. When Dave and Paul returned the borrowed sleigh, they had taken along one of Mary's pies as a thank you. From then on, whenever the Father was visiting his parishioners in the Udney area, he usually found a reason to drop by the Stone farm to say hi and of course chat over tea and pie. His second love was horses, draft horses in particular, and inevitably after tea, he and Dave would find their way to the barn to visit Dave's "boys," his prized Clydesdales, Atlas and Hercules.

"David, I'd like you to meet Father McCartney. He's just joined me at St. Columbkille's and I expect that he will replace me someday. I have been showing him around the Parish."

Mary must have heard the car and had come to kitchen door to meet them. "Hurry up and come inside where it's warm before you catch your death, Father!"

The group gathered around the kitchen table. The tea had been poured and the pie set out.

"Mary, David, I want you to know how sorry I am for your trouble."

"Thank you Father," answered Mary.

"How is Susan?"

"As well as can be expected. She and Becca have gone next door to gather the eggs and collect a few of Susan's things. She will stay with us until Paul returns, or…"

"He's a good lad Mary, strong and smart. He'll come home."

"It's hard Father. So many have been killed or are missing like Paul."

"Yes, but many more are safe and have come home. When I heard the news, I lit a candle for Paul and when you go to Christmas Eve Service tomorrow night, look to the south. When I light the cross atop St. Columbkille's, it will be there to guide him too to safety, just as it was ten years ago. Now Father McCartney have you ever tasted finer apple pie? Don't dally though. The temperature is dropping and that means there's a storm on the way. We'll need to leave for home soon and I want David to introduce you to his magnificent horses before we leave."

†

Paul sat in a wheelchair in the Adjutant's office at the RAF Base in Ipswich. It was the nearest base with a hospital and resident doctor and Charles Goodman had ordered the WAAF driver from the Air Ministry to take him here to report in and get his leg attended to. However, Paul had insisted on speaking with the Adjutant before being treated.

"Now let me see if I have this all correct Airman Stone. You are with the 166th stationed at Kirmington. Your Lancaster bomber was attacked and disabled on a mission over Holland. You were forced to bail out and were rescued by the Dutch underground and a British intelligence agent, a Charles Goodman, who hid you under a haystack. Then you and Goodman were smuggled aboard a Dutch fishing trawler, which rendezvoused with a British Navy patrol boat in the North Sea and returned you both to England early this morning."

Paul nodded, "That's about it."

"Indeed, I should think so! Remarkable, quite remarkable! Well, welcome back Airman Stone, bloody good show! While you are getting that leg attended to I'll ring up Kirmington and file a preliminary report. As soon as I know the status of your crewmates, I will let you know. Corporal, take this man to the infirmary."

†

"Well Paul," said the doctor, as the nurse was putting the finishing touches on the fresh dressing covering his wound, "it was slivers of plastic from your turret causing the infection, but they're out now. Once the antibiotic gets to work that leg of yours will heal as good as new. It is going to smart when the local anesthetic wears off, but I can give you something for the pain. And despite your eye's multicoloured appearance your vision seems unimpaired; but you probably did have a concussion. All in all you have come through rather well."

"I should say so!" interjected the Staff Sergeant who had just entered the treatment area. "Good news all 'round airman. I reached my counterpart, Simmons, at Kirmington. He tells me your aircraft made it back, just barely. Apparently the whole tail section fell off over the Channel and they just made landfall. They crashlanded amongst a herd of sheep in a field near Fiskerton. There were some minor injuries (none to the sheep), but everybody walked away. Your Lanc, though, is pranged. She'll never fly again. Your mates are all on 'survivor leave,' celebrating Christmas as best they can. But we don't know what to do about you."

"Why?"

"Well, officially you are still missing in action. Flight Sergeant Simmons will file a report immediately, but it will take at least a week for the Air Ministry staff to process it and inform your family that you are safe."

His family! Paul had forgotten that they would already have been informed of his status. "Flight Sergeant can I send a telegram to Canada?"

"Sorry lad, but no personal messages. There's a war on you know! Official communications only."

Paul knew he was right. There was no way to contact his family before Christmas to let them know he was alive and well.

Dr. Brown spoke up. "You can stay here, spend Christmas with us and then report back to Kirmington and celebrate the New Year with your mates." Then another voice was heard from.

"Hi Doc. I see you are keeping busy as usual. He's a good one son, do what he says!"

A tall, lanky figure dressed in civilian clothes but wearing a battered flying cap strode into the room.

"Sorry to interrupt Doc. Have you got those magic pills of yours ready for me? I can't be falling asleep half way across the North Atlantic."

Dr. Brown removed a small vial from his coat pocket and handed it over. "You be careful with these Buzz."

"Doc, you know I only use these on the overnighters—and maybe sometimes after we've hoisted a few too many."

"That's what I'm afraid of. What are you flying this time Buzz?"

"I caught a good one Doc; a long range Liberator. Takin' a bunch of Ferry Command fellas back to Canada for their next pick-up. They're ferrying over a dozen new Lancs a week, now that Avro's Victory Air plant in Toronto is in full production. The 'met' report looks good; tail winds all the way. We should make Gander by tomorrow and if the weather there holds, I'll be home in Toronto for Christmas Eve."

Paul interjected, "Did you say Toronto, by Christmas Eve?"

"If all goes well," said the pilot.

"Have you got room for a passenger?"

"Who's this Doc?"

"Airman Stone is a Canadian. He was shot down over Holland. He escaped and arrived on my doorstep about three hours ago. He's trying to get home for Christmas. Paul this is Buzz Thompson. Former bush pilot in your country, now assigned to the RCAF's Ferry Command. One of our finest, even if he does say so himself."

"Well, thanks. Is he fit Doc?"

"I'm not sure anyone is fit to fly with you Buzz. But give him a seat forward and keep him warm. He'll make it."

"OK! Stone, the more the merrier! Grab your kit and let's go. Take off is in twenty minutes."

Paul turned to the Flight Sergeant with a silent appeal.

"Well, it's rather irregular; but it is Christmas, you are on survivor leave and carrying orders to report to Canada anyway so... I don't see why not. Off you go Stone. I'll inform your commanding officer. We can't do much about your uniform, but..." He called an airman in from the hallway. "Corporal, find a forage cap and service overcoat for Airman Stone. He can't arrive home for Christmas looking like a refugee."

†

The flight across the North Atlantic was uneventful and Paul slept most of the way. They had touched down at Gander ahead of schedule. After refueling, Montreal was their next stop and Buzz delivered the Ferry Command crews to Dorval as promised. The veteran pilot's plan to have them both home for Christmas was on track, until the weather changed dramatically. The tail end of a lake effect snow storm swept into Central Ontario and flying conditions in the Toronto area deteriorated. But Buzz, a stubborn old bush pilot, wasn't about to let a little snow stop him. Despite poor visibility and an icy runway, he managed to land safely at RCAF Base Downsview in Toronto before it was closed.

Paul's first priority was to call home but the storm had blanketed Central Ontario. When he tried to telephone from the base the operator informed him that all lines north were down. There was no more time to waste. Buzz had ordered a taxi to take himself home and on the way he dropped Paul at Union Station.

Paul recognized the locomotive as soon as he stepped on the platform. Canadian Pacific Engine 1230 had brought him home to Udney on the Toronto to Washago run many times before. But he was surprised that on Christmas Eve there was just one car attached and no caboose.

He heard no call to board, but the train's whistle sounded and it began to pull out. He had not come this far to be left behind. Hobbling as fast as he could he reached the car, managed to grab the railing at the rear steps and swung onboard.

Paul collapsed into the rear seat, fighting to get his breath. His injured leg was throbbing badly and he hoped that he hadn't torn the stitches. It was hard to believe he had left England just a day ago. He looked at his watch; twenty-six hours to be exact. He had done it. He would be home for Christmas!

Paul stood to remove his coat and looked around. This car was clearly different from those he usually rode. It was a parlour car. There was a single passenger seated alone in a booth about midway and the front half of the car was curtained off. The curtain opened and a porter in a white dinner jacket emerged. He saw Paul immediately and came hurrying down the aisle toward him. He did not look pleased.

"What are you doing here?" he said officiously.

Paul was taken aback. "I'm traveling to Udney. I didn't have time to buy a ticket, but I will settle up with the station-master there when I get off."

"That will be difficult to do sir. This train will not be stopping at Udney."

†

Mary stood in the centre of the middle aisle at Udney United Church and nodded her head with satisfaction. The Christmas decorations were beautiful. The church smelled of freshly cut pine and the crimson bows on the newly hung wreathes would welcome worshipers to tonight's Christmas Eve service. Susan had finished arranging the white gifts under the Christmas tree and Becca was putting the final touches on the nativity scene. It had been a long but satisfying day.

Susan had seemed her usual self at breakfast, but it was clear from the dark circles under her eyes that she had not slept well. No matter, she joined in when Mary and Becca set out to help decorate the church and deliver some of the items they had prepared for the Christmas Eve supper. Busy was good and there really was nothing else they could do but wait and hope. She called to the girls.

"Well done ladies! Now we need to get home and changed for church."

Becca and Susan joined her. She hugged them both then took each by a hand and they walked together toward the rear. As they approached the exit doors her eyes fell on the small chalkboards hung on either side. One was draped in black; the other in white. One read, "Killed in Action" and had seven names listed. The other read "Missing," and it had just one. It was a solemn reminder that Paul might never again be home for Christmas. She squeezed the hands she held a little harder and they both responded. "There's always hope," said Becca. "And faith," added Susan. "Amen," thought Mary.

†

"What? What do you mean we're not stopping in Udney!"

"This is a private car, sir. It's on an express run to Washago, where it will be joined to the Transcanada Special when it passes later tonight. You should not be here."

"But it's got to stop at Udney. I've just returned from overseas and I'm hoping to get home for Christmas."

"William, what is it?" said a deep voice.

It was a voice of authority. It belonged to the only other passenger on board. Paul had noted him before, seated in the booth in the middle of the car. Even from a distance you could tell that he was a man of substance. An expensive looking overcoat hung from a hook beside him and a matching fedora was set on the rack above. He wore a suit which seemed well cut and freshly pressed and the stiff white collar of his shirt rose above the jacket's lapel. He had a good head of hair, full and startlingly white. Now that he had turned to address the porter,

Paul noted the man's piercing blue eyes and the strong set of his jaw. The porter hurried forward, spoke quietly to the man and returned.

"Mr. Gordon has asked if you would care to join him. He is the President of CPR's Ontario operations. This is his car."

William took Paul's coat and escorted him to the booth.

The man stood and extended his hand. "Welcome son. I'm Thomas Gordon."

Paul noted the firm handshake. "Airman Paul Stone, sir."

"Please sit down. Would you like some refreshment?"

"Yes, thank you sir."

"William, the usual please, for two. Now Paul, why are you on my train? From the look of your eye and the state of your uniform you must have quite a story to tell. Let's hear it."

While Paul was telling his tale, William returned with tea and a plate of cheese and crackers. Mr. Gordon was an attentive and knowledgeable listener. Indeed, he too was a veteran, having flown in the Great War. He was fascinated with the scope of the current air war. They were approaching Brechin before Paul finished his tale. William cleared the dishes and delivered a tray with a crystal decanter and two glasses. Gordon handed him a note in return. "William, please deliver this to the engineer."

Gordon poured a full measure into each glass and gave one to Paul, raising his own in a toast. "Merry Christmas Paul! This train will be stopping in Udney. Welcome home! Now tell me more about these Lancasters. They must be a magnificent aircraft!"

Paul stepped gingerly down to the platform. Almost immediately the air brakes hissed and then released. Steam billowed from beneath the engine. The huge drive wheels spun furiously, then engaged and with puffs of white smoke burping from its stack the locomotive slowly began to chuff on its way. He looked to the brightly lit windows of the passenger car. Its lone passenger was watching him from above. Paul raised his arm in a silent salute to his benefactor. Mr. Gordon nodded in response, then turned back to reading his reports. The red lights at the rear of the train soon disappeared into the darkness.

The storm had blown over, but a few flakes were still drifting down, sparkling in the glow of the platform lights. It was now a brisk winter night, cold enough to cause the snow on the platform to crunch underfoot. He looked eastward. The moon was up and a thick bank of cloud was chasing it across the sky.

Although the platform was lit, the light was off in Mr. Graham's office. No one appeared to be on duty. With no passenger trains expected until late tomorrow, he would be at church with the rest of the community. The lobby door wasn't locked and Paul stepped inside. The room was empty, but the wood stove had been stoked and the air was warm and dry. He crossed the room, opened the back door and stepped out to the rear platform. The United Church was less than a mile away. Its steeple made it the tallest structure in Udney. He could see its stained glass windows below, multicoloured panes glowing warmly in welcome. The whole community would be there for Christmas Eve service and the supper to follow. Paul turned up the collar of his overcoat, pulled it a little more tightly around his neck, descended the steps, thrust his hands deep in its pockets and began to walk. As he approached, the sound of many voices raised together in song reached his ears. He had missed that singing.

Once in the yard he noted a familiar odour: the scent of horses and manure. On special occasions some families still traveled to church by horse and sleigh, and particularly with the rationing of gasoline many seemed to have done so this year. He was certain that the Stone family's team of Clydesdales would be there and he spotted them immediately. Atlas and Hercules were standing quietly, still hitched to the sleigh and tethered to a post. Their golden brown backs were already coated with a light covering of snow. Paul went to them and they recognized him immediately. Stamping their feathered hooves in welcome they tossed their magnificent heads, flaring their nostrils and snorting clouds into the air.

"Hello boys, long time no see." He stroked their velvety muzzles and their ears pricked in response, huge hooves rising and falling in anticipation of a run.

"Easy fellas easy," he admonished. "I've got to say hello to the folks first." The great beasts calmed. The singing ceased and Paul could hear the shuffling and murmuring of the congregation as they retook their seats in the pews. Reverend Campbell began to speak.

Paul limped to the stairs and by pushing off with his good leg and using the hand rail for support he was able to climb the steps to the front door. He stepped inside and hung his coat on a vacant hook in the entrance hall. He took a moment to look at himself and was not pleased with what he saw. His uniform was a mess. In addition to the blood, oil and water stains, one pant leg was torn and several tunic buttons were missing. Three more steps up to inner doors, then Paul paused and waited for a break in the Reverend's sermon.

"... and Dear God protect them as they stand in harm's way to protect us. And finally Lord, please be especially vigilant for those missing in action, and in particular our native son Paul Stone."

Paul could wait no longer; he pushed open the inner door and stepped quietly inside.

"Paul Stone?" repeated Reverend Campbell. "Paul Stone!" he said again and emphasized his words by pointing. "Paul!"

The congregation turned as one and there was a stunned silence as they recognized the uniformed figure standing at the rear.

Susan's joyous cry broke the spell. She left the pew and ran as Paul limped toward her. They met in a crushing embrace. People began clapping and cheering and the organist struck up an impromptu chorus of Ode To Joy.

Wiping away her tears with one hand, Susan used the other to lead Paul to the Stone family pew. Becca and Mary hugged him together and buried their faces in his shoulders to hide their tears. David Stone stood silent. His brother Bill beamed beside him. Paul and his father locked eyes over the heads of their women.

"Hi Dad!" said Paul, and Dave smiled. "Welcome home son!"

Reverend Campbell called for order and after a few moments it was restored.

"Dear Lord, please forgive me. When I was delivering my entreaty, I did not expect it to be answered so quickly. Let us pray. Lord, we thank you for your kindness, mercy, and indeed swiftness, in returning this lost lamb to our fold. May your goodness and grace continue to be with all who tonight still stand in harm's way. Amen." He drew a breath.

"And now I invite you all to join us for our Christmas Eve supper. Susan and Paul, will you please lead the way?"

When they reached the exit doors, Susan stopped. Paul saw his name printed on the white draped chalkboard. Susan reached out and carefully erased it. Against all odds, her husband had made it home for Christmas.

Our Christmas Carol

MARY STONE TIGHTENED THE RED BOW putting the finishing touch on the last package and set it with the others she had prepared. The guest room at the Stone family farm doubled as the sewing room, but this morning it was also serving as a gift shop. The bed, chair and much of the floor were covered with packages containing items she had made or collected for the Udney United Church's Christmas gift drive. The packages were destined for delivery today, Christmas Eve, along with food hampers, to less fortunate families in their community. The mug of tea Becca left on the table beside her, before going to the barn, was still warm. Mary sat back in her rocking chair, took a sip and began to muse.

1946 had been a very good year for the Stone families. During WW II she and her husband Dave considered themselves fortunate to have maintained the operation of the family's farms, while their son Paul was overseas and their daughter Becca attended school in Guelph. This year Paul had been discharged from his post-war duties with the Royal Canadian Air Force and returned to rejoin his wife Susan in time for spring planting on their neighboring farm. He and his father picked up where they left off and the Stone farms were again flourishing. The fighting was over, the troops were home and many others, fleeing war-ravaged Europe, had come to Canada seeking a new beginning. The demand for meat, milk and produce had increased accordingly and the Stone farms were back in full production.

Becca had graduated from the School of Veterinary Studies at the University of Guelph and accepted a position as an assistant to local veterinarian Dr. Robert Williams. She was working out of Doctor Bob's office in Brechin and had returned home to live in her room on the farm. Mary was thankful that all her family was now back living in the Udney community and Dave was happy to have Paul home and Becca as a "live in" vet! He joked that he now had two vets at home.

But best of all, she was soon to be a grandmother! Paul and Susan were expecting a child early in the new year. Yes, she was a fortunate woman; blessed with a loving husband, wonderful children, a dear daughter-in-law and a grandchild on the way.

Even the weather had cooperated. It had been a summer of sunshine, with the right amount of rain at the right times. The result was a rich and bountiful harvest.

However, with the onset of winter Mother Nature had become less temperate. Mary glanced out the window beside her. It had snowed on Remembrance Day and several storms followed, covering the land early in its annual blanket of winter white. Then just days ago freezing rain drenched the area. Tree branches snapped under the weight of the ice build up. Power and telephone lines were downed. Roof tops, out-buildings and the snow covered fields were crusted with a thick coating of clear ice. Although services had been restored, temperatures had remained below freezing and the ice had not yet melted. Even now the morning sun was reflecting off the surface of the Stone's drive-yard, which resembled a skating rink, and the fence and surrounding outbuildings still wore crystal coats. Every post and eave glistened with ice. It was a beautiful sight, but a hazard for those who had to travel. Although the highways had been plowed and sanded, the untreated side-roads were still slick with a thick layer of ice. The concessions and lines were treacherous and most locals were avoiding travel. These conditions would make it difficult to deliver the parcels the Udney United Church was preparing for needy families. Even getting to tonight's church supper and Christmas Eve service could be a challenge.

But as usual the Stone family had a plan for coping. Paul would use his horse drawn cutter to deliver the gifts today and transport the family to church later.

He knew his team's weight on steel shod hooves and the cutter's sharp runners would provide all the traction he would need to get the job done. Mary knew also that Paul wanted to show off a little. Dave's heavy team, Atlas and Hercules, had carried out such duties in past years. But, like father like son, Paul now had his own magnificent Clydesdales and was anxious to display their might and skill.

Mary heard the team coming up the laneway and went to the window. Thor and Odin came into view drawing the cutter, tossing their heads and snorting vaporous clouds into the frigid morning air. Paul held the reins and his wife Susan sat beside him smiling and waving at Becca and Dave, who had come out of the barn to greet them. Paul guided the horses in a wide circle and brought the cutter to a stop near the rear of the house.

Mary put down her mug and headed for the back door. As usual, it would be up to her to restore order and organize the busy day ahead. She arrived on the back porch in time to see Becca release Susan from a hug and watch the pair launch into an animated conversation. Mary could guess the topic: the pending births. Susan's bulky winter clothing could not hide the advanced state of her pregnancy and that would be the first subject for discussion. Becca wasn't pregnant, but her horse Star was. In fact Star was overdue. As a veterinarian Becca knew this was not unusual for a mare delivering her first foal, but she was still nervous that all would go well. Susan was following Star's pregnancy almost as closely as her own. Star's foal was to be her Christmas gift from Becca.

Paul and Dave were at the head of the team, each holding a horse by the bridle and stroking noses. They were of course comparing and sharing their views on Paul's new "boys" and Dave's old "boys," and discussing heavy horses in general. Mary shivered and pulled her cardigan more tightly across her chest. It was time to call the group to order.

"Alright Stone family, come over here and get your marching orders."

The group assembled and she continued. "Susan, I would like you to help me with the baking for the church supper tonight and you need to stay warm, so please go inside right away." Susan smiled and started into the kitchen, pausing to hug her mother-in-law on the way by.

Mary continued, "Becca I can use your help with the baking too, but first we need to bring the Christmas packages out so the men can load the cutter and get on their way. Dave, once you and Paul leave here, your first stop is the railway station to pick up the donations Charlie Graham has collected. He telephoned this morning to say he is ready for you. Then deliver the load to the church where Reverend Campbell and some volunteers will sort and repack for each family. You'll get your list of deliveries and you two can work out the best route to follow. Now, no dawdling this year to sample Christmas cheer and talk horses, crops and hockey! You need to be back here by dark to get cleaned up and ready to get the girls, me and our baking to the church hall on time… any questions?"

Paul snapped to, saluted his mother with military precision and replied, "No Ma'am!" Everyone laughed, even Mary.

"Well, then let's get to it. Becca please bring some wood for the stove with you."

Although Mary now had an electric range for everyday use, she could not bear to part with her beloved McClary wood stove. It still heated the kitchen when needed and in her opinion always provided just the right temperature for baking. The McClary would be well used today. She re-entered the house. Becca cracked some ice off the pile of wood next to the porch, selected a number of pieces and followed her mother into the kitchen.

†

Dave smiled as he surveyed the scene from his seat atop the cutter. It was a beautiful winter morning. He and Paul had carried out this pleasant task before, sometimes in the pickup truck, but whenever possible with a team and cutter. The wondrous look on the children's faces when two huge horses arrived at their homes pulling a sleigh full of Christmas gifts, always reminded him of the true spirit of the season. He glanced at his son holding the reins beside him and enjoyed the joy in his expression. Six years ago Paul had been a teenager attending school and helping his Dad on the farm. Now he was a young man, a veteran of war, married, with a child on the way, and working his own farm in partnership with his father. Dave's chest swelled with pride.

Even the horses were in high spirits. As they made their way down the driveway their steel shod hooves crushed the icy surface beneath. Chips exploded outward, sparkling like diamonds in the morning sun. Some clung to the horses' legs, decorating their caramel stockings with frozen rhinestones. Thor and Odin were just three years old and had only been Paul's horses since spring. Dave had been with Paul when he'd purchased them from the Olaffson farm. Old Ole had good stock and bred carefully. Dave was confident that Paul's horses would round into a great team. But they still had some growing to do and would need a lot more training before they rivaled Atlas and Hercules at the Fall Fair trials. They turned onto the concession road toward the Udney Depot where station-master Charlie Graham would be waiting.

The road was still ice covered and crowned in the centre but there was no other traffic in sight so Paul guided the horses into the middle, letting the runners straddle the ridge. Thor and Odin didn't seem to be having any trouble with the footing and pulled away smartly.

"How many miles do you figure we will do today Dad?"

Dave replied, "I spoke with Reverend Campbell after the Service last Sunday. He had ten families on the list then and may have added a few since."

"Wow! That's up from the last time I helped."

"It's not as bad as it seems," Dave explained. "Many of the families had men away during the war and as you know some did not return. They just haven't been able to recover yet. And we have a few new families this year. The Dutch and Polish refugees that immigrated here haven't quite caught on to Canadian farming yet, but they will. It is our community's responsibility to give them a hand up until they do. Based on what the Reverend told me, I expect we will do twenty miles or more, round-trip. Depending on how many stops and how long we spend at each, it will probably take all day. I see you brought some feed for the horses and you know we will get offers of food and drink at every farm, so I'm thinking we will be hard pressed to get home by dark."

Paul responded, "Mum will skin us alive if we make her late for the church supper, and I know Susan wants to go home to rest before we leave."

"Is everything all right? Is she not feeling well?" Dave asked.

"She's very tired and little anxious about the baby. She and Mum really got into canning and preserving this year, and she has spent a lot of time sewing baby clothes and preparing the nursery, then along came Christmas and..."

"What do you mean, anxious about the baby?"

"Oh, Doc Gordon says everything is fine and on time. He thinks your grandchild will arrive in about two weeks. But Susan and I are both a little nervous about having a newborn to care for. Her mum is ready come up from the city by train as soon as the baby is born. I am certain she and Mum will have everything under control. In fact, I bet you and I will be exiled to your place with visiting rights only for a while. Were you this nervous when you and Mum were expecting me?"

Dave chuckled, "You bet we were. We were living in Toronto then and both of our families were living up here, so we were truly on our own. Having a city hospital nearby was a big help, but we weren't sure what to expect as new parents when we got you home. But we must have done something right. Look at you now!"

Paul elbowed his father's shoulder in response and then snapped the reins. "Hi Thor, up Odin, let's go, we've got a long day ahead of us!" The Clydesdales pricked their ears and pulled away.

†

Mary's kitchen was wonderfully warm and the delicious aroma of baking bread wrapped around the three women like a comforter. Susan had finished rolling out the dough for the pies. Becca had prepared the pie plates and set them out to be filled. Three large bowls of fruit filling, apple, cherry and peach, stood ready to be spooned into the shells. Mary added some quartered logs to the fire and the McClary crackled with heat. She tapped the thermostat and nodded with satisfaction at the reading. She had planned for eight pies.

"Ladies, the oven will be ready soon. Becca, I know you are anxious to get down to the barn to be with Star so let's get the assembly line started. You can fill the plates." Then she added her usual caution. "Please be careful not to overfill them. Susan perhaps you can keep her under control."

The young women smiled and nodded at each other. Becca's habit of overloading the pies had become a Stone family tradition; Christmas baking wouldn't be the same without at least a few bubbling over.

"Once that is done, Becca you are free to go and Susan, you and I will top them and get them into the oven."

"Thanks Mum," said Becca. "Star was acting very uneasy this morning; pacing and stamping. She knows something is going on but this being her first foal, she is not sure what it is. Dad and I moved her to the big stall at the far end, well away from Atlas and Hercules. Susan, I'm pretty sure your Christmas present is going to arrive today."

"Can I come down later and stand watch with you? I have never seen a baby horse born and I can't wait to see if mine will be a boy or a girl."

"You mean you want to see if her foal is a colt or filly."

Susan had been raised in the city and when she married Paul she had gone from office worker to farm wife in the course of just a few days. It was a big change but with Mary's help she had made a remarkable transition to becoming a country woman. However, she still had some things to learn about life on the farm.

"Sure you can join me; we'll hold hands," answered Becca. "Delivering Star's foal will be a learning experience for me too. I read the sections in the text but our class only saw a film of a normal equine birth. So this will be a first for Star and us. Are you going to come Mum?"

Mary shook her head. "I'll leave that to the two of you and Star. I've got enough to do to get ready for tonight. Although the supper is a little later this year, because of the midnight service, I will have to pack up everything for the ride to the church and get cleaned up early. The men will get gabbing and be late as usual, so I will need to get your father cleaned up and dressed when he returns. But first things first. Becca, finish filling the shells. Susan please cut that dough into strips so I can begin topping the pies. Let's get to it."

†

A half hour later Becca left for the barn. The sun was at its zenith, but a breeze had sprung up out of the west making the air feel colder than it really was. The pathway to the barn was very icy and she made a mental note to spread stove ashes to improve traction. She opened the small door and stepped through.

Becca loved the warmth and smell of the barn in early winter; scented with a mix of second cut hay, blended with the odour of oiled leather harness and the smell of horses. It enveloped her and made her feel welcome. Sunlight streamed through the cracks and knot holes in the barn boards and motes of dust danced, suspended in golden beams of light.

When she approached Star's stall she saw immediately signs that foaling was imminent. The young mare was rubbing her side quarter against the wall of the stall and her chestnut coat was glistening with sweat. When she turned and moved toward Becca, it was obvious that the foal had shifted toward her hindquarters and, just as described in the textbook, the muscles on either side of Star's tail were beginning to roll and flex. She came close enough for Becca to rub her muzzle. "It's okay girl. You don't understand what's going on do you?"

Star's head bobbed in response to her mistress' reassuring voice and tone, but her huge brown eyes rolled and her tail swished furiously confirming her unease. She moved away again. Becca was now certain the foal would be delivered that afternoon. It was time to prepare. She let herself into the stall and took from her pocket the cloth strips she had cut earlier. She would first wrap Star's tail to keep it out of way, just in case human help was needed, and then go up to the house and call Dr. Williams. Although Star was Becca's horse, she was Doc's patient and he wanted to observe both his patient and his new assistant during the birth. She finished the wrapping, stroked Star's neck, spoke reassuringly and with a final hug left the stall and returned to the farmhouse.

†

"Well that's the lot," said Reverend Campbell. "People have been very generous again this year." The cutter was now piled high with food hampers and gifts. The curled nose of an upended toboggan towered above the back of Dave's head and two bicycles were tied to the cutter's rear panel. The good Reverend removed a watch from his vest pocket and flipped open the cover. It was almost 11:30. "Will you join us for lunch before you head out?"

Dave shook his head. "Thanks but we have a long way to go, a lot of stops and not much time. Mary has already warned us not to be late because she has to get to the church hall early to deliver her pies and help with the preparations for the supper."

"Well, far be it from me to cause any upset to your lovely wife, particularly when I am looking forward to a slice of her pie to fortify me for tonight's service. Travel safely and remember to invite everyone to the supper and service. Remember the meal is later this year, at 8:30, and then we'll sing some carols and let the Sunday school children open some gifts from under the tree, before the service."

"Don't worry Reverend, the schedule is cemented into my memory; Mary has seen to that."

The minister smiled. "I bet it is, and in mine too apparently. Thank you again for delivering the hampers and I will see you later tonight. God bless and keep you."

†

Becca and Susan were just stepping off the back porch on their way to the barn when Doc Williams' pickup came clanking into the drive-yard. A stout older man exited the vehicle. He was wearing his trademark English flat cap with a bounty of snow white hair escaping from beneath. His overcoat was open, displaying his usual working attire, a tweed jacket, vest, collared shirt and tie and wool trousers. His well worn Wellington boots, however, were less than pristine, so it appeared that this was not his first stop of the day.

"Hi Doctor Bob," said Becca, "glad you made it."

Doctor of veterinary medicine, Robert Williams smiled and returned her greeting. "So am I Becca! If it hadn't been for the weight of the grain sacks in the back and the chains on the rear tires, my truck and I would probably be in a ditch somewhere. The roads are still in bad shape."

He continued, "Hello Susan. Becca tells me you have a special interest in this foal."

"That's right Dr. Williams. Becca has been teaching me to ride on Star. I really enjoyed it and wanted to get my own horse. Star's foal is Becca's gift to me. I will be able to raise it and train it, with Paul and Becca's help, so we can all ride together."

"That sounds like a great plan. From what Becca said when she rang me, you'll soon know if your horse will be a colt or filly. Here, give me your arm Susan, this path is quite slippery. Becca, please lead the way."

When the trio arrived at the barn they found Star already down on her right side in the straw, with her head turned, neck stretching back toward her hindquarters. Her time had come.

Susan spoke first. "What do we do now?"

"Hopefully nothing," replied the vet. "Horses were foaling long before humans were around to help. We just need to let nature take its course and be ready to step in if there are any complications."

He noted Star's wrapped tail and the bucket of warm water Becca had set nearby. "I see you are prepared just in case."

Star whinnied softly; her breathing had become heavier and her muscles were clearly straining. The foal was being born. A foreleg tipped with a tiny hoof appeared first and the nose of the foal followed and lay alongside it. But then things came to a halt. Star was still straining but there was no progress.

"What's wrong?" asked Susan.

"Can you tell her Becca?" said Doc, as he began to remove his jacket and roll up his sleeves.

Becca responded immediately. "The other foreleg is stuck. It must be folded over. Those sharp little hooves need to puncture the amniotic sac to free the foal. Star needs help."

Doc stopped his preparations. "Can you do it?"

Becca nodded, "I think so."

She rinsed her hands in the water, Doc opened the stall gate and Becca approached Star slowly. She could see the fear in her horse's eyes and spoke reassuringly. She felt carefully in beside the foal's neck, quickly found the little hoof, freed it, and laid it alongside its mate. Star responded. Almost immediately her water broke and in a rush of fluid the foal slipped out fully and lay on the straw. It was a filly. Becca backed away slowly, quietly praising her mare, and exited the stall.

The next steps were up to Star. She seemed surprised to find herself sharing her stall with another creature and if a horse can look bewildered it was her. But she started to hunch her body even further around and began to caress and clean her baby. So far so good.

Susan could hardly contain herself. "Oh Becca, she's beautiful. Her coat is the colour of honey. Will she stay that shade?"

Becca smiled, "She should. Her sire was a dark palomino, about the colour you see now." Star struggled to her feet and continued grooming her baby. The group stood talking softly while watching mother and foal interact and waiting for the next miracle. It was not long in coming. The little filly began struggling to stand. Once, twice, three times; she tried so hard, but each effort resulted in a monumental collapse into an untidy tangle of legs.

Star nickered and the foal tried again and again, until finally she stood on four wobbly legs, gazing around at her strange new world. But not for long. Instinct prevailed and she staggered between her mother's legs and began to take suck. Star accepted this new sensation calmly; standing still, she turned her head and long neck to nuzzle and caress her foal. They had bonded.

The girls clapped their hands silently and cheered softly. Doc Williams smiled and patted Becca on the shoulder. "Couldn't have done better myself young lady. Well done!"

He turned to Susan. "They're both going to be fine and I am sure she will grow to be a beautiful companion for you. Now, I have to get on my way, but I can't leave until you name her."

Susan laughed. "I really haven't thought of many names. I needed to know if it was a boy or... I mean a filly or a colt, and I wanted to see her colour and markings. But having her arrive on Christmas Eve has given me an idea. She's my Christmas angel. I am going to name her 'Angel.'"

"That's a wonderful name, Susan!" said Becca, and hugged her hard.

"Good choice," agreed Dr. Williams "Now, I must go."

"Susan, why don't you go up to the house with Doctor Bob. You've had enough excitement for one day and should rest before we clean up for church. The men won't be back for at least another hour. You can tell Mum the news and then lie down for a while in the guestroom. I'll stay here, lay some fresh straw, make sure Star has enough feed and water and keep an eye on Angel. Off you go! I'll be up in a while."

Doctor Williams and Susan clung to each other for mutual support as they made their way up the icy path to the farmhouse. Susan stopped by the woodpile and waved goodbye as his pickup pulled out of the yard. The sun was now low on the horizon. Paul would be gone for a while yet and she was looking forward to some tea and a nap before tonight's activities. She turned to step up onto the porch and then remembered the Stone family rule.

"Whenever you come in the back door, bring a few pieces of wood for the stoves." She reached toward the woodpile. Suddenly her feet slipped out from under her. She tried to steady herself with one hand on the pile, but it too slipped. She toppled sideways, struck her head against the steps of the verandah and fell to the ground. Susan felt a sharp pain above right her eye and reached up to touch it. Then the darkness closed around her.

"Hi up!" Paul snapped the reins, Thor and Odin pulled away and the cutter slid out of the McLeod's driveway and on to the fourth line. They had finished their deliveries. It would be a straight run to the concession road, a right turn and about five miles to home from there. It shouldn't take them more than a half hour with an empty sleigh. They would still be about an hour late, but it had been worth it and he was sure his mother would understand. She always did. But darkness had fallen, so he knew their wives would be concerned.

"Did you hang the lanterns on the back Dad?"

"I can remember when I used to ask you that question," replied Dave. "It is a good thing you thought to bring them. One on each side and two on the back should do the trick. Anyway, I doubt that we will meet anyone on the road tonight. Your team has done well today, Paul. I was afraid they might be a little skittish when the children started to gather around, but they were fine. That's a good sign if you plan to show them or enter the 'pull' at the Fair next year."

"Did you see the look on the de Munnik kids' faces when you put them up on the horse's backs? I doubt they saw any horses that size in the Netherlands. Knowing they will have warm clothes and some gifts under their Christmas tree is worth our effort, but seeing the joy in their eyes as they hugged the necks of their new friends was a bonus."

A light snow had begun to fall and was powdering the surface of the road. It didn't seem to be affecting the team's traction but with the weight gone the cutter began fishtailing a little as they approached the concession.

Paul pulled back on the reins, slowing to make the turn. "Whoa boys, easy now," and the team responded.

Suddenly his dad tapped his shoulder and pointed to the other side of the road. "Red lights in the ditch. That's a car. Somebody didn't make the turn."

Paul followed his dad's line. "Looks like it. And there's the driver on the shoulder waving."

Dave exclaimed, "I think that's Doctor Gordon. I'd recognize that fedora anywhere. He must have an emergency to be out on the road tonight."

They made the turn and Paul brought the cutter to a stop.

Dave called out, "Hi Doc!" jumped down and hurried over to the tall figure who had stopped waving and now seemed to be supporting his right arm with his left hand. They exchanged a few words, then Dave picked up the small black bag beside the doctor, escorted him to the sleigh and helped him up onto the seat.

"What happened Doc?" asked Paul. "Are you hurt?"

His father spoke first. "Paul, we have to get going right away!"

"Aren't we going to pull Doc out? I've got the tow rope with me and the boys can handle the job easily. I know we're late but this can be our excuse."

Dave responded in a tense but firm voice. "Paul, the doctor has an emergency and we need to get him there immediately. Get the sleigh moving and he will tell you about it on the way."

"Okay! Hi Thor, up Odin, let's go boys!" He snapped the reins and the horses pulled away with a will. "Where are we heading, Doc?"

"To your parents' farm, there's been an accident."

"What!"

"Paul," said Dave, "it's Susan, she's had a fall. Your mother called and Doctor Gordon was on..."

Paul cut his father off. "Is she all right Doc? What did Mum say?"

"Paul, all I know is that she fell and hit her head. Apparently she had been unconscious for a while when they found her, but she's awake now."

"Is the baby..."

"Let's not jump to any conclusions. The sooner we get there the sooner I can examine her; so you concentrate on getting us there quickly, but safely. Meanwhile, Dave will you please take my scarf and use it to make a sling for my right arm. When the steering wheel spun I jammed my wrist. I don't think it's broken but it hurts like the devil."

Dave followed the doctor's instructions while Paul stared straight ahead over the backs of his team. He held the reins firmly, fighting the desire to use them to urge the horses to greater speed. They would be home soon enough, but now his feeling of Christmas joy had been replaced by uncertainty and fear for his wife and their unborn child.

†

Mary sat in the chair beside Susan who was propped up in bed. She was holding a cold pack to the ugly swelling on her daughter-in-law's forehead. The cut over Susan's eye had stopped bleeding. Mary had dressed it with small band-aid, but her eyes were still a little glassy and they slowly began to close.

Mary spoke sharply. "Oh no you don't! You need to stay awake. Doc Gordon said he wanted you bright eyed and sitting up when he got here. He should be arriving any minute now. Tell me about Angel again."

In her mind Mary was wondering what was taking the doctor so long. She had called over an hour ago and he said he would leave right away. Becca came to the door of the guest room.

"Would you two like some tea? I just brewed a fresh pot."

Susan nodded her head and Mary replied, "Thank you Becca that would be nice."

Becca looked at Susan. "Well Sis, have you had any more contractions?"

When her mother discovered Susan lying semi-conscious by the back steps and called Becca from the barn to help, their first concern was Susan's head injury. That changed quickly when Susan began to respond to their questions. Her first words chilled Mary's heart.

"Mum, I think my water has broken," and if any confirmation was needed, moments later when they were helping Susan to her feet, she doubled over with the pain of her first contraction.

Susan smiled weakly, "No, just the three so far. Mum says there is lots of time yet. I just wish Doctor Gordon would hurry up and get here."

She turned her head toward the window. Although the lace curtain was drawn she could see the bright glow of the farm safety lamp lighting up the yard. "Where is Paul? It's dark and he and Dad should be home by now."

As if on cue, they heard Shep barking, followed by the jingle of sleigh bells as the cutter and team entered the drive-yard.

"They're home!" cried Becca. "Your tea will have to wait!" And she hurried to the back door to meet them.

†

"Whoa boys!" Paul brought the cutter to a halt and handed the reins to his father.

"Dad, please look after the team while I take Doc Gordon into the house."

Dave nodded, "Go!"

Paul jumped down and hurried around to help the doctor from the cutter. Becca met them at the porch steps.

"Dr. Gordon, thank goodness you're here!"

"Where is Susan?"

"She's in the guest room. Mother is with her." Becca held the door and the group entered into the warmth of the kitchen. Becca took the doctor's coat, Paul helped him remove his overshoes and began to follow him to the guest room.

"You stay here," ordered the doctor. "You and your sister can exchange information while I wash up and examine Susan."

"But Doc I…"

"Stay here," he repeated. "I will be able to answer your questions after I see Susan and talk to your mother."

Paul hung his coat and reluctantly took a seat at the kitchen table. "Sis, what happened?"

Becca lifted the coffee pot from the stove and held it at the ready. "I'm not sure Paul. She was coming back from the barn and fell near the woodpile. It looks like she hit her head on the porch steps. She must have been unconscious for a while before Mum found her, but she was awake and talking when we helped her into the house. She has a nasty looking swelling and a small cut above her right eye."

"That's not too bad."

"Well, perhaps," replied Becca haltingly, "but that's not all of it."

"What do you mean?"

"Paul, Susan's water broke and she's having contractions. She's gone into labour."

"But, it's too soon!"

"Maybe not; let's not jump to conclusions," replied Becca. "We need to wait until Dr. Gordon finishes his examination. Here, have a coffee."

Becca poured. Paul added milk but except for the clink of his spoon striking the ceramic mug there was silence while he stirred and contemplated the swirling clouds in his coffee.

"I'll take a coffee down to Dad in a minute but first tell me how you ended up with Dr. Gordon on your cutter."

Paul told her what had happened. "Good timing!" she marveled, "or perhaps a little divine intervention? What's wrong with his arm?"

"Doc jammed his wrist when his car went into the ditch. He's not sure if it is a sprain or a fracture, but regardless, he can't use it."

Becca nodded, then her eyes brightened. "Hey, I forgot. I do have some good news! Star had her foal; a filly. Susan was with me through the whole birth. She named her new horse Angel."

Paul listened, but did not really hear. He sipped his coffee, his gaze fixed on the hallway leading to the guest room. Suddenly the door opened. Dr. Gordon stepped into the hallway and strode toward the kitchen.

"Becca, I sure would like a cup of that coffee, black as usual please." He took a chair beside Paul and placed his injured right forearm on the table. "And if it's not too much trouble could you make up an ice pack for my wrist?"

"Right away, Doctor."

"Paul, I have some good news. I don't think Susan has a concussion. She is alert and other than a band-aid and the cold pack your mother has applied to her forehead, there is not much else to be done. Now, for the surprising news. I expect you will be a father before morning."

"But..." Doc Gordon held up his hand.

"I know, this is sooner than you expected. Susan's fall did, I think, have something to do with it. But based on my examination, I don't think the baby is premature, just a little early and anxious to join the family for Christmas."

"Shouldn't we take Susan to the hospital?"

"Normally I would say yes, but given the road conditions," he pointed to the ice pack on his arm, "and the timing of Susan's contractions, we might not make it. I do not want to have to deliver this baby in the back seat of a car. I understand your father was born in that guest room, so I guess it is good enough to welcome his grandchild."

"But..."

"Paul, everything seems fine. It should be a normal birth. Like you, Susan is a little worried about the timing, but she knows there is nothing she can do now but have a healthy baby. That's what she is focusing on. You can go in now and visit for a few minutes."

Paul almost ran down the hall to the guest room.

"Becca, Susan tells me that Star foaled this afternoon and that you assisted with the birth."

"Well, a little," she replied, then went on to explain what had happened.

Dr. Gordon smiled, "Good hands, eh? Well, you need to be prepared to help with this birth too. I can't deliver a baby with one hand."

"But... Doctor Gordon, I can't."

"Becca, I will be the eyes and give the instructions. You will be the hands when the time comes." Seeing the shocked look on her face he continued. "I have discussed it with Susan and your mother and they both have great confidence in you. Now please go and wash very thoroughly and then join me in the guest room."

†

Paul entered the barn carrying two cups of coffee. Dave had just finished watering the horses; he turned to greet his son, bucket in hand.

"Paul! How's Susan?"

Paul told his father all he knew and Dave, like Doc Gordon, reassured him. "Paul, Doc Gordon has followed Susan's pregnancy from the beginning. He's the best and I trust him. And with your mother and Becca to assist, this baby will get all the help it needs to arrive safe and sound."

Paul smiled and nodded but did not seem fully convinced.

"It looks like all we can now do is wait. As I recall, I spent five hours pacing in the waiting room at Toronto Western Hospital, while you took your time in appearing."

Dave was about to sip his coffee when he paused, walked over to the door, reached up and removed something from its hiding place on the beam above. He set his coffee cup down on the stall post and pulled to remove the cork from the flask of amber liquid he had acquired. "Don't tell your mother!"

Dave poured a measure into his own cup and a bit more than that in to his son's.

He raised his mug. "To my grandchild. May he or she arrive swiftly and safely!"

Paul clinked mugs with his father. "Cheers to that!"

Dave pointed to Star and her foal. "Paul, do you remember the Christmas Eve we got lost in the storm and Star went missing? Now that was a Christmas to remember. If I recall you thought it was your fault and I was blaming myself because..."

Paul nodded. He did indeed remember but his thoughts were on the drama unfolding on this Christmas Eve.

†

Susan had been struggling for the past four hours to bring her baby into the world. The last contraction had been long and very strong. Mary wiped her daughter-in-law's brow with a damp cloth.

"You're doing find Susan," said Doctor Gordon. "Almost there."

"Becca, are you ready?" The next contraction came quickly.

†

Dave and Paul sat at the kitchen table. Dave had just finished his second piece of pie, but Paul's first piece still sat, half eaten, on his plate. It had been over an hour since Mary had come out to report progress. They could hear the sounds of Susan's struggle but could only wait and hope for a positive outcome. Dave tried to lighten the mood.

"Ted Reeve said in his column yesterday that he thinks the Leafs have a good chance to win the Cup this year. Apps and Broda are back in form and 'Teeder' Kennedy and that rookie Meeker are really playing well together."

Paul responded, "It'll still come down to their defence. If Barilko is as good as they say we just might see the Cup back in the Gardens."

The guest room door opened. Mary hurried up the hallway with a basin in her hand. She rinsed it in the sink, took a kettle from the back burner of the stove and filled it with water. She tested the temperature with her finger, nodded, turned to leave and saw the questioning looks on their faces. "Everything's fine! I don't think it will be long now." Then she spotted the half eaten pie on Paul's plate.

"Those pies are for the church..." Then she caught herself, looked at the clock and smiled. It was almost midnight. "Well, I guess it doesn't matter much now; enjoy!"

Then she added, "Paul, the stove needs more wood; Dave, please make another pot of tea." With that she set off back down the hallway.

David and Paul carried out their duties, freshened their coffee and returned to their seats at the table. It was not the Christmas Eve they had planned.

The grandfather clock in the parlour chimed twelve times.

"Merry Christmas, son!"

"Merry Christmas, Dad."

The next sound they heard was the unmistakeable squall of a baby crying. Paul almost jumped out of his seat to go but his father restrained him. "Wait."

The minutes passed like hours. Then Doctor Gordon appeared with Mary in tow and entered the kitchen. "Paul, Susan would like to introduce you to someone."

Paul hurried to see his wife. Mary put her arms around her husband's neck from behind, kissed his ear and said softly, "Congratulations Grandpa. We have a beautiful granddaughter."

Dr. Gordon added, "Indeed, and both mother and daughter are doing well! Mary, I am famished. May I have a slice of that pie? David, is there any coffee left?"

Paul sat on the edge of the bed holding his daughter cradled in his arms. "She's beautiful honey."

Becca cut in, "Of course she is. She's my niece! Now give her back to her mother."

Paul carefully complied. Susan sat propped up in bed and put her baby to her breast. "Thank you Becca. Your steady hands were the first to hold her."

From her seat by the window Becca said, "Susan you did all the work and Dr. Gordon gave the directions. All I did was catch her."

"Thanks Sis!" said Paul. "I guess that makes two successful births for you today. While you two were busy, Dad and I visited Star and her foal and that mother and daughter team is doing well too. I really like her name. I hope Angel suits her temperament as well as it does her birth-date."

"Speaking of names," said Becca, "what are you going to..." She suddenly broke off her comment, drew aside the window curtain and looked out in amazement. The drive-yard was beginning to fill with people. Some were holding lighted candles. It was Reverend Campbell and what seemed to be the whole congregation of their church.

Mary, Dave and Dr. Gordon entered the room. "It looks like the party line has been busy," said Mary. "I knew when I called Doctor Gordon the word would get out, but I didn't expect..."

"Silent night, holy night, all is calm, all is bright..." The choir's voices were clear and sweet in the midnight air.

"What a beautiful carol," sighed Mary. "The whole community has come to welcome your Christmas child. But wait, she doesn't have a name yet. Does she? Susan, Paul, have you chosen one?"

Susan said, "We talked about some for both boys and girls, but this sort of changes things." She turned and whispered in Paul's ear. He smiled broadly and nodded in agreement.

Susan continued. "It's Christmas and we have been blessed with a beautiful child. To honour the season, her name is Carol."

The room was silent for a moment, then there were smiles, hugs and handshakes all round.

Mary took over. "Dave please go out and invite those wonderful people in for pie and tea and whatever else we have to drink. Becca, will you help Susan prepare? Paul, please take Doctor Gordon into the parlour and get organized. As soon as everyone is ready, we will introduce them to *our* Christmas Carol."

The Gift of Giving

MIKE MILLER STOOD LEANING AGAINST THE OPEN GATE of the milking stall, smiling as he watched his six year old sister Jennifer play with the puppies. Their border collie, Shadow, had littered three weeks ago and her pups, Salt, Pepper and Spice, as named by Jenni, were eager to explore the world around them. Jenni lay on her stomach in the straw beside them while each vied for her attention, forcing their wet little noses under her chin, snuffling and licking her face and fingers. She giggled and pushed them gently away, but they were relentless in their attack. Shadow sat quietly nearby, tail wagging slowly, keeping a close eye on her charges.

It was good to see a smile on his little sister's face and hear joy in her laughter. The Miller family had not had much to smile about lately, and with Christmas just a day away Mike knew that the spirit of the season would be overshadowed by his parents' struggle just to make ends meet.

1948 had been a difficult year for the Millers and 1949 was not shaping up to be any better. When Canada went to war Mike was only two years old. The family lived in Oshawa and his father Tom was working for General Motors. Building automobiles was not a wartime priority and the family moved to Malton near Toronto where both his Dad and his mother Barbara worked for the A. V. Roe aircraft company building Lancaster bombers. Jenni was born in 1942. When the war ended so did the building of warplanes and the Millers returned to Oshawa. Post war sales of cars were poor and General Motors cut back. After several lay-offs his father was forced to seek other employment. He had been raised on a farm, so when he saw the advertisement for a live-in hired hand for a farm he decided to return to his rural roots.

The Miller family moved again, this time to the small community of Udney, just southeast of Orillia, to work for the Eriksons. The Erikson farm was a 100 acre beef and cash crop operation. Lars and Greta Erikson and their son Jaan had made a success of it.

But Jaan had been killed overseas during the war. The Eriksons carried on, but when Mr. Erikson was crippled in a tractor accident, they were forced to seek hired help. The Millers moved on to the Erikson farm in late June of 1947.

Twelve year old Mike was at first upset about having to leave his friends and change schools yet again, but the switch from city to country life worked out better than he expected. He enjoyed farm life, especially working with the Erikson's herd dog Shadow, rounding up the cattle. In September he and Jenni enrolled at Public School (PS) #9 in Udney.

There were just two teachers and only sixty-four students for the eight grades. Jenni's teacher, Miss Speiran, taught grades one to four and the other, Mr. Hunter, looked after the grade five to eight pupils. Jenni fit in immediately and after some initial hazing by a few of the older boys Mike found his place. Being a good athlete and helping the PS #9 team win the annual softball tournament against the schools from Lawrence, Fair Valley and Brechin had helped him to gain acceptance.

Things at the farm, however, did not go so well. The operation had deteriorated during the war and when Mr. Erikson was injured the bills had piled up. Following the fall cattle sales in 1948 there was not enough cash to pay the Millers, the bills and the mortgage too. The bank

foreclosed and both the Eriksons and Millers were forced to leave the farm. With two children in school and the birth of a third expected in November, Mike's parents decided to try and stay in Udney. They bought the old Wilson place that sat on a couple of acres of land about a mile from the village. It consisted of a small single story house, an outbuilding for storage and a corral for livestock. It was in poor condition and available for a very low price.

Mike's dad was sure that with their garden, a milk cow, some chickens and hiring himself out to nearby farms, combined with part-time winter work at plants in Orillia, they could make a go of it. Their parting gift from the Eriksons was the cow Thistle and the faithful farm dog Shadow.

Mike and his dad had worked hard to repair and upgrade their new house. They couldn't afford electricity, but the woodstove served well for both cooking and heating, and kerosene lamps provided the light they needed. They renovated and expanded the shed to accommodate the chickens and Thistle. It took a lot of work and some sacrifice but the old Wilson place was now the Miller's home. The newest member of the family, his baby sister Hope, arrived just after they moved, putting an additional strain on the family budget. His father Tom had been able to get some "daily hire" work in Orillia; however, it was still going to be a very lean Christmas.

Thistle stirred in the stall beside him, halting Mike's musing. With a loud bawl and a toss of her head against the restraining ropes, she was reminding him it was time to let her out. Thistle came by her name honestly. Although a good milk producer, she was temperamental and had to be handled carefully. Prior to milking her, he always secured the rear restraints before placing the pail and stool in the stall. But he was finished now and had removed those restraints, preparatory to releasing Thistle from the stall and returning her to the corral. It was time to get to it.

"Jenni, leave the pups be for awhile and start collecting eggs, while I separate the cream. Mum needs both for breakfast."

"Ok Mike! Now you three stay put," ordered Jenni as she left the pups and crossed behind Mike to get her egg basket. She picked it up and turned back for one last look at her little friends. Mike turned to hang the restraining straps near the stall. Then Pepper decided to abandon Salt and Spice and wander away from their bed. He set out on wobbly legs, tottering toward Jenni.

"Get back there you," ordered Jenni. She pointed and started toward the errant pup. Thistle had had enough. She bawled again and shifted her weight angrily. Suddenly Mike realized what was coming. He turned and saw Jenni walking toward the puppy.

"Jenni no!" he cried, just as Thistle let go with a lethal kick of her hind legs.

But Shadow was faster. Her instincts had warned her too.

She leaped forward and knocked Jenni down and away from those flying hooves. Mike heard the sickening sound of a hoof striking flesh and bone as Shadow took the brunt of Thistle's kick. The faithful dog flew sideways, landed heavily on the straw strewn floor. She lay deathly still.

Mike slammed the stall door shut behind Thistle and ran to Jenni. She was crying, but already struggling to stand, still clutching her egg basket. Bits of straw were stuck in her hair and clinging to her clothing. As far as Mike could tell she was unhurt, just upset. Jenni wiped the tears from her eyes with her sleeve.

"Mike, what happened?"

He started brushing the straw from her hair and clothes. "Thistle decided to act up and you almost got kicked. Shadow knocked you out of the way and ..."

"Shadow!" cried Jenni. She ran to the dog, dropped by its side and began stroking her head. Her hand came away bloodied. "Mike, she's hurt!"

He moved Jenni gently aside. "You go and look after the puppies. I'll see to Shadow." Shadow was indeed hurt. A quick examination showed cuts and bleeding indicating she had taken the blow on her left side and head. She was unconscious, but still breathing. Shadow was going to need more treatment than he could provide. He knew someone who might be able to help, but he would have to get Shadow to her.

†

Doctor of Veterinary Medicine Rebecca Stone sat slumped in her chair staring at the piles of paperwork on her desk. She had at least separated the original hodgepodge into appropriate categories; bills to pay, invoices to mail, reports to be completed, supplies to be ordered etc. Although they had taught her about this aspect of being a "vet" at the University of Guelph, the reality of it was just beginning to sink in. When she had trained by assisting Dr. Robert Williams she treated animals and collected and assessed blood and tissue samples. Dr. Bob had an office assistant who handled all of the administrative work. All he had to do was sign the cheques. When Dr. Williams went into semi-retirement and offered most of his practice to her she accepted eagerly and opened her own facility in Udney. It consisted of some office space with a single treatment room and a kennel area for dogs, cats and some of the other small creatures that needed to stay post treatment. It wasn't lavish but would do for the time being.

However, she was a one person show. For much of each day she was on the road in her battered old Ford pickup visiting farms and treating animals. She never seemed to be able to find the time to deal with the business aspect of her practice and do the chores too. Speaking of chores, the kennel was awaiting attention. Her last patients had been removed by their owners earlier in the day, to spend Christmas with their families. The kennel needed to be washed down, disinfected and readied for use after the holiday. The paperwork would just have to wait.

It was the day before Christmas and she had planned to take the afternoon off and spend Christmas Eve with her family. She rolled her chair away from the desk, took off her long white treatment coat and donned her work jacket. She was about to stuff her feet into the waiting pair of Wellingtons when she heard a loud and insistent knocking at the front door. She was not expecting anyone.

"Just a minute!" she called and walked toward the door.

The knocking continued. "I'm coming!" She opened it to find a boy standing on the porch cradling a dog in his arms. She knew them both. Mike Miller was clearly distraught and his dog Shadow lay unmoving against his chest.

"Mike what is it, what's wrong with Shadow?"

"Thistle kicked her! She's unconscious and having trouble breathing. Can you help her Dr. Stone?"

Becca knew Shadow. The Eriksons' farm adjoined her parents. The Stones' herd-dog Shep had sired Shadow's pups and Becca had visited the Miller place after their birth to find mother and pups doing well.

"Bring her in Michael. Follow me to the treatment room."

Michael laid Shadow carefully on the stainless steel top of the examination table and stepped back. Becca began her examination. Shadow was unconscious and her breathing was laboured, but her pulse was steady and her heart was beating strongly.

"Did you see what happened, Mike?"

Mike described the incident and noted that it was Shadow's left side that had taken the brunt of the blow. Becca nodded and continued her diagnosis by touch. Then she took a penlight and checked each of Shadow's eyes.

"Is she going to be alright Dr. Stone?"

"I don't know yet Mike, but I might be able to help with her breathing problem. It feels like a couple of her ribs have been dislocated and are pressing on her lungs. I think I can put them back in place."

"Will that cost a lot Dr. Stone? I don't have any money, but..."

Becca paused and then smiled as she thought of a solution. "Mike, I was just about to begin cleaning the kennel when you arrived. Why don't you start on that job while I look after Shadow."

"Sure thing!" replied Mike. He stroked Shadow's head gently and then left to start his task. Becca watched the door close behind him and then turned her attention to her patient. "Well Shadow, let's see what I can do about your ribs." Her gentle hands began their work.

†

Mary Stone and her daughter-in-law Susan stood side by side on the back porch of the original Stone farm house watching their men prepare for the annual Christmas run, delivering baskets of food and gifts to less fortunate families in their community.

Mary's granddaughter Carol, their Christmas baby who would be two years old tomorrow, stood between them, each holding one of her tiny mittened hands. Mary's husband Dave and her son Paul, Susan's husband, were in high spirits because this year they could use the horses to make the gift run. Atlas and Hercules, David's magnificent team of Clydesdales stood quietly in the drive-yard while he and Paul finished the harnessing. Mother Nature had cooperated and delivered a heavy fall of snow over the last two days. Last year a December thaw had turned the side roads and concessions to mud and they had been forced to use Paul's pickup for their holiday deliveries.

But arriving by truck just wasn't the same. Nothing buoyed their own Christmas spirit more than seeing the joy and amazement on children's faces when a sleigh full of gifts drawn by two huge horses arrived at their houses on Christmas Eve. Today the roads were still snow-packed and that meant that the sleigh and heavy horse team could be used to make the journey this year. Mary called to them.

"Now remember, pick up the extra parcels from Charlie Graham at the train station, then go to the church. Reverend Campbell has a group of helpers there ready to sort, tag and help you load."

"Yes Mother!" responded Paul. He was used to this annual giving of instructions and knew what was coming next.

"And no dawdling, talking hockey and horses and sampling the newest batches of Christmas cheer at every stop. You need to be back in time to clean up and get ready to take us to church; particularly this year Dave. The Sunday school teacher has a birthday cake for your granddaughter, and you definitely don't want to miss your brother Bill playing Santa for the little ones. Barring an emergency, Becca should be joining us too. And Dave, be sure to stop at John Moore's office. The papers are ready for pick-up; just in time I might add."

"Yes dear," Dave responded bemusedly.

He and Paul climbed on board and took their seats. Dave took the reins and snapped them. "Hi up boys!" Atlas and Hercules pricked their ears, took the weight on their collars and pulled away. They too were eager for a run. They surged out of the yard and down the drive, hooves splashing in the snow, leaving a frosty exhaust in their wake.

Mary watched them go and then turned to her daughter-in-law.

"Well, they're off, and I have no doubt they will, as usual, be late in returning. C'mon Susan, let's get started with our baking. We at least can be sure our pies are ready, and be dressed and waiting if and when they do manage to get back on time."

Susan smiled at her mother-in-law's predictable comments. This was her fourth Christmas as a member of the Stone family. Two years ago baby Carol's birth, on Christmas Eve, had prevented their attendance at the Christmas Eve supper and service, but despite their husbands' adventures, the men had never yet been late for the dinner.

"Alright Mum, let's get busy. Come on Carol."

She scooped up her daughter and followed Mary into the warmth of the Stone farm kitchen.

†

Mike returned to the treatment room to find Dr. Stone putting the finishing touches on the stitches she had sewn to close the cut on Shadow's head.

"How is she Doc?"

"Well Mike, I was able to relieve the pressure the rib injury was putting on her lungs. She is breathing normally now and I disinfected and stitched the cut on her head. But she is still unconscious. I am certain Shadow has a concussion. The blow to her head has caused her brain to swell inside her skull. That is why she's in a coma."

"Will she get better?"

"That depends, Mike. If the swelling is not too severe it will subside and she will wake up and be okay. If it increases then she'll, well..."

"Is there anything we can do Doctor Stone?"

"No Mike. It's up to Shadow now. But if you give me a hand we can make her more comfortable in the kennel and let nature take its course."

Mike carried Shadow and Becca handled the doors.

He lay Shadow on a straw bed in one of the cages and Becca placed a bowl of water near her. Mike gently stroked her head just above the wound.

"Get better girl," he said softly, and they left Shadow to her fate.

Once back in the office Becca surveyed the piles of papers on her desk and then glanced at the wall clock. It was nearing noon.

"Mike, I am going to call it a day. I'll come back and check on Shadow before I go to the church supper and service tonight. We should know by then. Would you like a ride home?"

Becca locked up while Mike loaded the toboggan he had used to transport Shadow into the bed of her pickup. During the trip Becca tried to lighten the mood.

"What do you have planned for the holidays Mike? I hear Mr. Hunter is holding practices for the school hockey team. Will you be trying out? What position do you play?"

"I won't be playing."

"What? Why not?"

"I don't have any skates. I've outgrown my old ones."

"Well, maybe Santa Claus will bring you some?"

Mike smiled, "That would be great, but right now I'd settle for Santa helping my dad to get home for Christmas with good news about a job."

Becca didn't reply but offered a sympathetic smile. She turned into the Millers' driveway and parked.

"May I come in and see baby Hope and the pups?"

Mike brightened, "Sure and maybe you can explain to Mum and Jenni about Shadow."

†

It was a wonderful winter morning. The bright sun climbing in the sky belied the sub zero cold. The trees had been dusted with new snow and sleeves of ice on the fence wires sparkled. Atlas and Hercules were enjoying the outing as much as Paul and Dave.

The two men sat tall, surveying the land they loved. Atlas and Hercules tossed their heads with joy, nostrils flaring, as they stepped out in tandem, hardly straining as they drew the sleigh along the snow-covered concession.

"Dad, what's this about papers at the lawyer's office?"

Dave smiled. "Remember when your mother and I bought the McIsaac farm? It was our chance to acquire more land right next to us and enabled you and Susan to have your own home."

Paul nodded.

"Well, we are doing the same for your sister. Becca needs her own place to live and do her veterinary work, so we made an offer on the Erikson farm. The bank wanted to sell it quickly and your mother is a tough negotiator. We got a great deal. It's Becca's Christmas gift and we've kept it a secret until the deal closed. An envelope with the deed will be waiting for her under the Christmas tree tomorrow morning. The bonus is ..."

"Becca won't farm it, but we can." Paul chuckled. "We'll use the extra land to increase our beef production, just like we were planning."

Dave nodded. "But with three farms, the cash crop, the dairy cows, feed crops and now more beef cattle, it will take a lot of extra work. Now that Stone Family Farms has become such a large operation we'll probably have to hire some help. Speaking of big operations we had better be quick about our visits this year. Reverend Campbell told me last week that the need was greater and we would have more stops. Thankfully donations are up too."

They turned onto the first line and the Canadian Pacific Railway depot came into sight. As they approached the platform station-master

Charlie Graham stepped out of his office and walked toward a pile of boxes being sorted by his assistant, Jimmy Blair.

"Paul, you help Jimmy load the sleigh while I pick up the papers across the street. When we get to the church Reverend Campbell and his helpers will fill the hampers and if we are lucky we'll get a bowl of Mrs. Campbell's soup to tide us over until dinner."

†

Becca parked her pickup in its usual spot in the Stone farm's drive-yard and sat musing in the warmth of the cab. She was troubled by what she had seen and heard at the Millers'. Barbara Miller had greeted her warmly and offered tea and cookies which Becca had declined. The house had just three rooms. Jenni and Mike shared one, their parents and Hope the other and the third was the kitchen, dining and living area all in one.

There was no indoor plumbing. But the common room was clean and tidy. The wood stove radiated a welcoming warmth and Hope and Jenni appeared well cared for. However, Barb Miller seemed very tired and worried. Becca brought them up to date on Shadow's condition, reassured Jenni and made a fuss over Hope and then the pups. But she left with a heavy heart and an idea forming in her mind. She exited the truck and gave old Shep, their long-serving herd-dog, a vigorous head rub when he trotted up to greet her.

"Hi boy. Your friend Shadow took quite a knock today and I hope she's going to be alright." She noted the tracks of the horses and sleigh leading down the driveway and smiled. Her dad and Paul had already left on their annual Christmas Eve mission. She entered the back door, hung her coat, hat and scarf in the mud room, kicked off her boots and stepped into her slippers.

When she opened the inner door and entered the kitchen she was immediately wrapped in the warmth and aroma of fresh baking. Her mother was bent at the waist removing something from the oven of her trusty McClary wood stove that she still used for her baking. Her sister-in-law Susan stood by, wearing oven mitts, ready to take the item and put it with the others on the cooling shelf. Carol sat snug in her high chair gurgling and pointing as she watched her mother and grandmother at work. She crowed "Becca!" when she saw her aunt.

"Hi Cutie-Carol! How are your Mum and Grandma doing with the baking? Will we have enough pies and bread for tonight's dinner?"

"Yes," Mary replied, "even without your help. I thought you were coming home early to overfill the pie shells, as usual?" Both Becca and Susan smiled at the jibe.

"Sorry Mum, I had a last minute emergency."

Becca related what had happened and brought her mother and Susan up to date on Shadow's condition and her visit to the Miller home.

"Mum, do you know if the Millers will be getting a hamper from the church?"

Susan replied, "I'm sure they aren't Becca. Barbara Miller was on the organizing committee with me. They were not on the list and it would've been embarrassing for her if anyone had suggested it. In fact, Barb donated a quilt she'd made and her husband Tom donated his labour to split a cord of wood for old Grandma MacGregor. Why do you ask?"

"Well, when I was there it was obvious they do not have very much. The house was clean and neat, Mike and Jenni seemed well cared for and baby Hope was a joy. But I know they could use some extra food over the holiday and I am sure that with three growing children they need clothes and boots and stuff. They had a Christmas tree, but there was nothing under it. I could hear the stress in Barbara's voice. She was clearly worried about Tom getting home by tonight and whether he had found work in Orillia. That's why they aren't going to tonight's church supper and service."

Both women looked to Mary. As if on cue all three smiled and nodded their heads.

Mary spoke. "Well girls, here is what we are going to do. Susan you must have..." and the planning began.

†

Although the sun was dipping toward the horizon Paul and Dave were for once on time. Their deliveries had gone well. As usual the children were the focus of each stop. Seeing wide-eyed boys and girls, some with legs too short to straddle, perched on the massive backs of Atlas and Hercules, waving to their parents with one hand, while clutching a candy cane in the other, was a sight that never failed to bring joy to their hearts. They knew the hampers and gifts they delivered were welcome and would be put to good use. They could not accept all the offers of refreshment but had consumed enough seasonal drink to lighten their mood. Paul was now handling the reins on the trip home while Dave enjoyed the ride.

"What do you think about the Leafs this year, Paul? Will it be a third Cup in a row?" Paul and his father were ardent Leaf supporters. They had never actually been to a game at the famous Maple Leaf Gardens. But every Saturday night they sat in the parlour, ears glued to the radio, living and dying with their team's success as described by Foster Hewitt's broadcast from the Gardens' gondola.

Paul smiled and replied carefully. "It'll be tough this year dad. Syl Apps has retired. Teeder Kennedy is the Captain now and Detroit, with Howe, Lindsay and Abel, looks awful tough. They should make the playoffs, but we'll see."

"Do you think Becca will be surprised with her Christmas Gift?"

"Well, you surprised me. I think Becca will be shocked. Renting in the village was a good way to get established, but she does need her own place to live and it will be perfect for her veterinary work."

Paul guided the team onto the county road. They would follow it through Udney and then make the final turn on the fourth line to their farms. They tugged the brims of their hats a little lower to shade their eyes as they were now facing directly into the sun. There was no other traffic in sight, automotive or horse drawn. But Dave spotted in the distance a lone figure on foot, head bowed, shoulders hunched against the cold, trudging toward Udney. As they drew closer Paul recognized the walker. It was Tom Miller. They pulled alongside.

"Whoa boys, easy now." Paul brought the sleigh to a halt.

"Merry Christmas, Tom," called Dave. "Would you like a ride?"

Tom turned to face them. His cheeks were ruddy, flushed from the cold, and his blue eyes were bright with wind tears.

"I surely would Dave." He handed up the small partially filled cloth bag he was carrying and climbed into the rear seat of the sleigh.

Paul snapped the reins. "Hi up! Let's go boys," and they were on their way again.

"Thanks fellas. I hitched a ride from Orillia as far as Uptergrove but I've been walking from there. It was cutting it close, but now I'll be home by dark. I haven't seen Barb or the kids since Sunday."

Not one for subtlety, Dave spoke up. "Were you working in town?"

Tom replied, "I got some daily-hire work at Otaco, but that ended yesterday when they banked the furnaces for the holidays. I stayed with friends until today, applying for jobs in the new year, but no one is hiring; even part-time. But I am sure something will turn up. What are you two up to?"

Dave explained their mission. Tom mentioned his wife's quilt and the wood he had split for Mrs. McGregor and then the talk turned to hockey and politics.

They dropped Tom Miller at the end of his driveway.

"Will we see you at church tonight, Tom?"

Tom shook his head. "We'll see, but I don't think so. I'll ask Barb but with the baby and me being away...you know. Thanks again, and please wish Mary and Susan a Merry Christmas from Barb and me."

As they pulled away Paul spoke quietly. "Dad, did you see the Red Shield stitched on Tom's bag?"

"I did, and if the Millers need help from The Salvation Army then things for them are tougher than I thought."

"Do you think there is there anything we can do to help?"

"Paul, Tom Miller is a hard worker and proud man. He will be very reluctant to accept charity. But I don't want to see our community lose the Miller family. There must be something we can do. Let's talk it over with the women when we get home. Stir up those horses son. Let's put on a little speed for the last mile."

Paul didn't have to be told twice and neither did the horses. The runners hissed with speed as their sleigh sped toward the warmth and welcome of the Stones' farmhouse.

Little did they know the women had done some planning of their own.

†

Mike finished stoking and stirring the Quebec heater in the far corner of the sitting area and then turned and surveyed the room. He had mixed feelings about what he saw.

Their small Christmas tree crouched in the opposite corner. He and Jenni had cut it themselves. It was short but had a good shape. The decorations were not fancy. Jenni had made some at school and then added a few homemade binder-twine strings of pop corn and cranberries. There were no lights, but the star that topped it was beautiful. Jenni had cut the shape from cardboard and covered it with silver paper saved from tea packages. Now it shone brightly in the flickering light of the kerosene lamps, reflecting the joy and hope of the season. There were even a few wrapped parcels under the tree. They had appeared shortly after his father returned from town. Would that there were more.

He looked toward Shadow's bed near the kitchen stove and saw Jenni sitting cross-legged beside it. She held a baby bottle half full of milk in one hand and Pepper, who was sucking lustily on the nipple, in the other. With no Shadow to feed them, cow's milk dispensed from one of Hope's discarded bottles was filling the void.

Salt and Spice, already satisfied, were curled up together, sound asleep. Would Shadow return to care for her pups?

And then his gaze turned toward the two figures sitting side by side at the kitchen table hunched over their cups, heads inches apart, talking together softly but earnestly. He couldn't hear their words but he knew the topic. His father had found no good prospects for work in Orillia in the new year. Would his family's Christmas present be yet another move?

"Enough!" he thought and began to walk toward the back door. He needed to bring in more wood and stoke the kitchen stove, which heated that end of the house. He had slipped on his boots and was reaching for his coat when from out in the yard he heard the sounds of bells jingling and voices laughing. There was a knock at the door.

He opened it.

"Merry Christmas!" said four voices, almost in unison. "May we come in?" In response Mike opened the door wider and looked to his parents.

His father nodded and five Stones, Dave, Mary, Susan, and Paul carrying little Carol stepped into the warmth of the Miller's kitchen. Mary Stone spoke up.

"Barbara, when Dave and Paul met Tom on the road he told them you might not be joining us for the dinner and service tonight. So we have decided to bring a little of our community's Christmas to you. Paul, don't just stand there. Give Carol to Susan and go and get what's in the sleigh."

Mike saw his father start to raise his hand in protest.

"Tom, put your hand down," said Mary Stone. "I am in charge, at least for the time being. Mike, you're already dressed so please give Paul a hand."

Mike followed Paul outside and found the Stone family's magnificent horses and sleigh standing in the drive-yard. It was piled with cardboard boxes, cloth bags and hampers.

"All of this for us?"

Paul just smiled and nodded. The two of them began to unload and carry everything into the house. By the time they'd made the last delivery, order had been at least partially restored. Mike's mother was examining the baby clothes and other items that Susan had brought, while Hope looked on from her high chair. Carol was sitting by Jenni who was trying to control the now wide awake puppies and Mary was in the kitchen filling the cupboard with canned and dry goods as fast she could unload the boxes. Several pies and a fresh turkey sat on the counter near the stove.

Dave Stone and Tom Miller were seated in chairs by the Christmas tree having an animated conversation. There was a lot of hand waving and head nodding and it ended with a firm handshake. Tom went to his wife and spoke quietly to her. Her face lit up and they hugged, hard. Dave Stone came to the kitchen and spoke to his wife.

"Tom says yes. He can start early in the new year and between Tom, Paul and I we will have the new place ready for Becca and spring planting too. Can we..."

"I already put the bottles in the icebox. You each get one, I repeat one, to celebrate, and then it's off to church."

Mike was still trying to take it all in when he heard the sound of jingling bells and a very loud "Ho! Ho! Ho!" at the door.

Jenni jumped to her feet. "Mike, it's Santa Claus, let him in!"

Mike opened the door and there he stood, whiskers and all, with a bag of toys slung over his shoulder.

"Thank you, Michael," he said. "I couldn't come down the chimneys with those fires burning so the door will have to do. I don't have much time. Jenni, I read your letter. You asked for a doll. Will this do?"

Santa took a beautifully dressed blonde blue eyed doll from his pack and handed it to her.

Jenni held the doll at arm's length and then hugged it to her chest. "Thank you Santa, she's just what I wanted."

Santa had a few other things in his bag for her, and while Jenni was occupied with her doll her father whisked them away for later placement under the tree.

Then Santa spoke to Mike. "I understand you too have a special Christmas wish, Michael. Come on now, speak up."

Mike was lost for words. He didn't want to spoil Jenni's fun by stumping Santa.

Then she spoke up! "He wants skates Santa, so he can play hockey!"

"Oh no," Mike thought.

Santa, though, seemed unfazed. He rummaged in his sack and pulled out a pair of CCM skates. "Will these do Michael?"

Mike's eyes opened wide. "How did you . . . ?"

"Santa always knows, Michael!"

Smiling, Mike took the skates, noting the thinly disguised scratches and scars on the boots and blades and the faded initials PS on the inside of the tendon guards.

"Thank you very much, Santa!" Mike smiled at the jolly old elf, then nodded slightly at Paul Stone who was standing by the Christmas tree. Paul replied with a smile and thumbs up.

"Now I must be going," said Santa. "I have a stop to make at the church before I finish the rest of my deliveries around the world. Merry Christmas!" and with a final jingle of his bells Santa took his leave.

Mary Stone spoke up. "Goodness yes, the dinner and service; we had best be on our way too." The Stone family gathered by the back door.

"Will you be joining us?" she added.

Barbara Miller gestured at the bounty around her. "No Mary. Hope is falling asleep, and your generosity has given us a very special Christmas Eve and left us with much to do."

Then Tom added, "But thanks to you folks you can count on us being there for sure next year. Merry Christmas!"

The Stones delivered a chorus of Christmas wishes in return and opened the door to depart. But their exit was blocked. Becca Stone stepped into the kitchen, then turned and beckoned. Shadow stepped into the light and began to limp toward her pups.

"Shadow!" cried Jenni and ran to hug her. "I took good care of them while you were gone."

Shadow snuffled in Jenni's ear and licked her face, then gingerly settled into her bed. Salt, Pepper and Spice wasted no time in cuddling in, eager for their mother's attention.

"Thank you Dr. Stone! Will she be okay now?"

"She'll be pretty sore for a while, but I think so Mike. Bring her to see me in a week or so. I'll check her over." Then she pointed to what Mike was holding. "I see you found some skates."

"Santa brought them!" announced Jenni, "and he brought me a doll!"

"I wonder how he knew?" smiled Dr. Stone. "Now, I must get going to church."

The Stone family was gathered in the Millers' drive-yard.

"Santa," said Becca, "there is a Sunday School class awaiting your arrival. Hop in my pickup and I'll drive you."

Her Uncle Bill nodded, climbed into the passenger seat and they were off.

Dave helped Mary and Susan up into the sleigh while Paul held the bundle that was Carol at the ready. Once Susan was settled in he passed their daughter up and joined them in the rear seat.

Dave called up the horses, flicked the reins and Atlas and Hercules pulled smartly away. There was no moon, but the night sky was crystal clear and the stars sparkled. It was a perfect night for a sleigh ride.

Once they made the turn onto the concession and set course for the church, Dave bunched the reins in one hand and put his arm around Mary .

"Well done, dear." He hugged her to him. "And Tom has agreed to start as our lead hand in January."

Mary smiled and pointed to the east. A star bigger and brighter than the others hung on the horizon. "Do you remember…"

Dave picked up her thought. "Our star of hope, the Cross atop St. Columbkille's Church. It was nice to give it a little help this year."

"Did you see the kids' faces when Santa arrived?" said Paul. "Jenni was shocked that Santa knew her name and was able to find her. When he handed her Becca's old doll her smile lit up the room. Mike kept up the façade for his sister's sake, but when Santa produced my old skates for him even he was surprised."

Susan said, "The look of love and appreciation in their parents' eyes will keep my heart warm until spring."

"It was a small and simple thing," added Mary, "a gift everyone can give. The gift of giving; the best gift of all."

A Community Christmas

THE STREAMLINED LOCOMOTIVE SAT SHROUDED IN SNOW, stalled at the Udney Station. The deep rumbling of its diesel engines signaled an eagerness to depart, but David Stone knew the train would not be leaving soon. The CPR line was blocked at the Monck Road crossing.

Dave too was idle. He sat slouched in the passenger seat of his daughter Becca's battered old Ford pickup. The engine was running, the wipers were barely keeping the windshield clear and the heater was struggling valiantly to warm the cab. With his injured left leg stretched across the seat, he had decided to stay warm and watch events unfold from his vantage point in the parking lot. For the last three days the Central Ontario snowbelt had been blanketed with a steady fall of snow. The community of Udney had received more than its fair share. Keeping farm drives and yards clear was an ongoing chore and road travel had become a slushy challenge. Yesterday, tired after a third session of plowing the yard and paths to the outbuildings, Dave had gotten careless, missed his step down from the tractor and badly twisted his knee. His wife Mary had applied ice and provided tea and sympathy.

With Christmas just two days away he was frustrated to be hobbled and using a cane. He should be helping his son Paul prepare the horses and cutter for tomorrow's annual delivery of Christmas cheer to area families, but instead he had been relegated to accompanying Becca on her pre-Christmas errands; one of which was to pick up a shipment of supplies for her veterinary practice. The CPR had bigger problems. Keeping the tracks clear of the unrelenting snow had contributed to an unfortunate and serious accident.

The CPR track plow clearing the route from Brechin to Washago had collided with a Simcoe County road plow at the Monck Road crossing near the junction with Highway #69. The steam locomotive and caboose unit pushing the plow had been derailed. They were now blocking the line and a significant stretch of track had been torn from its bed. Fortunately there had been just minor injuries to the two crews.

The fact that the streamliner stalled at the station was a "special" with only one car added to the crisis.

Dave hated to leave the warmth of the truck but, given what he could see transpiring on the platform, it looked like his friend Charlie could use some support.

Station-master, Charles Graham, was faced with several problems, not the least of which was the protestations of the imposing man confronting him on the station platform. The tone and volume of the stranger's voice combined with his finger pointing made it clear that delaying his departure was unacceptable and he expected Charlie to do something about it. Standing near the pair was an attractive middle-aged woman, wearing a long fur coat and matching hat. A tall young man who appeared to be accompanying them stood nearby. The woman seemed embarrassed by the debate and placed her hand on the older man's arm to calm him. Dave noted that the young man appeared indifferent to the discussion and was focusing his attention on a slight figure unloading packages from the baggage car. That was his daughter, Becca. Although she was dressed in overalls, a red and black plaid jacket and wearing Wellingtons, the blonde hair spilling from under the billed cap and her bright smile left no doubt that she was an attractive young women.

Noting her struggle to push the loaded baggage cart along the snow covered platform, the young man left to go to her aid. Together they managed to force the cart to edge of the loading dock near the waiting pickup. A congratulatory handshake followed.

Becca called to him. "Dad, Mum told you to stay off that leg!"

Dave didn't bother to answer and continued to make his way toward the group. By the time he arrived Becca and her helper had joined them. Station-master Graham was addressing the group.

"Fortunately, Mr. Slate, there is a fully equipped works depot in Washago. Despite the approaching holiday they still have a crew on duty and all of the needed equipment is on hand. The crane car has already left the yard and they are recruiting local men to assist our CPR workers in clearing the wreckage and laying new track."

"Have they given you an estimate, station-master, of how long we will be delayed?"

"No sir, but the supervisor on site feels, if the weather conditions do not worsen, they can have at least one track open soon. Perhaps by Christmas Day. He has recommended that you stay here, ready to leave on a few hours notice. Now that your special train has been delayed, traffic control in Toronto has telegraphed to inform me that they have decided to join your car to the transcontinental in Washago. You will get to your meetings in Winnipeg, albeit a few days later than planned."

"Stay here? We can't stay here...," he glanced at the station sign, "in uh...Udney. Our car is not equipped for sleeping and preparing meals."

"Perhaps there is accommodation here in the village dear?" interjected the woman.

"I am sorry Mrs. Slate, there is no inn in Udney. I have arranged for the train crew to stay in the basement at the United Church, but I hardly think bunking with them appropriate for your family."

"Indeed, that is not acceptable," blustered the man.

Dave Stone interrupted the irate speaker. "Charlie, perhaps you could introduce our visitors and then we can discuss how we might help them?"

"Yes, of course Dave. This is Mr. Alexander Slate, his wife Isabelle and their son Richard. Mr. Slate is the CPR's Vice-President in charge of freight. Mr. Slate, this is David Stone, one of our leading citizens."

Dave tipped his hat, "Mrs. Slate," nodded "Richard," and extended his hand to the imposing figure in tweed. "Welcome to Udney Mr. Slate. I am sorry that the circumstances of our meeting are not more pleasant."

Alexander Slate took Dave's hand in a very firm grip, which Dave returned. Their eyes locked as they measured each other; industry leader meeting community leader.

"I too am sorry about the circumstances Mr. Stone. Another peril of having too many unmarked crossings and whistle stops like aah… Udney, slowing our heavy freight. Do you have a suggestion regarding accommodation?"

Dave didn't, but he noted Becca signaling him.

"My apologies dear. May I present my daughter, Rebecca Stone. Your son was kind enough to assist her with her shipment of supplies for her veterinary practice."

Both men tipped their caps and Mrs. Slate extended her hand. "My, a veterinarian. Well, I am pleased to meet you Rebecca."

"Please call me Becca, everyone does. Dad, we are the solution. You and Mum have a big and very empty home. I know that except for some last minute wrapping and baking Mum is ready for Christmas. The Slates can stay with you. Richard can have Paul's old room and Mr. and Mrs. Slate can take the guest room. And if the track should be repaired and their train cleared to leave, they are just a few minutes away."

"Oh, we couldn't possibly impose on you, especially at Christmas," protested Mrs. Slate.

Dave Stone looked surprised and then thoughtful. Becca never ceased to amaze him.

"Hospitality is not an imposition Mrs. Slate, and in our community helping others in times of need is a given. My wife Mary enjoys Christmas company and will welcome you for as long as need be."

Then pointing to his cane he continued, "Besides looking after you will keep her from fussing over me."

"Becca," he nodded toward the station office, "please telephone your mother and tell her we have guests."

Becca smiled and left the group to accomplish her task. Her father couldn't see the look of relief on her face or know that besides being hospitable, she had an ulterior motive in inviting the Slates. She had a secret to keep and in order to do so her father had to be kept at home and away from her farm.

†

Mary Stone hung up the telephone and smiled. Christmas always seemed to provide challenges or bring surprises to the Stone family. Apparently Christmas 1950 would be no different; they would be having house guests for a few days. She was a little tired, but her morning chores were done and she was ready to accommodate.

Last night's meeting of the new School Board had run very late. It was her first since being elected trustee and there had been much to do. The most contentious issue had been the decision to close several local schools, including Udney's own PS #9, and transfer the children to the big new school being built in Brechin. Loss of community identity, travel by school bus and staffing had been major concerns; but in the end the decision had been made. She scanned the kitchen for tidiness and then went into the parlour. The Christmas tree in the corner was unlit but the decorations reflected the light from the lamp on the end-table and the colourful wrapping on the presents under the tree made a festive display. The Quebec heater was warming the room and the odour of wood smoke added to the ambience. She spotted David's tea mug still sitting on the table beside his chair near the radio. He rarely remembered to take it to the kitchen after the listening to the morning agricultural reports. She collected it and on her way to the kitchen looked into the sewing room. It was a mess; but a controlled one. Gifts, both wrapped and unwrapped, ribbon, bows and festive paper lay scattered about. She had yet to finish preparing some items for Paul and Dave to deliver on their Christmas cheer run tomorrow. She knew the bathroom and the bedrooms upstairs were immaculate. The Stones were ready to host.

The kitchen window overlooked the drive-yard and she saw the truck arrive. Becca was driving and a woman in a fur hat was in the cab with her. Her David, an older man in an expensive looking overcoat, holding his fedora on his head with a gloved hand, and a younger man wearing neither hat nor gloves were seated in the truck bed. She hung her apron on the hook by the stove, smoothed her dress with her hands, and went to greet her guests.

After much stamping of feet to remove the clinging snow, boots and overshoes were stowed and coats and hats were hung in the mud room. With just two small bags the Slates were traveling light and the group gathered in the kitchen. Becca had taken care of the introductions.

"Thank you Mrs. Stone for your hospitality, particularly on such short notice," said Isabelle.

"Indeed!" added Alexander Slate.

"You are most welcome," Mary replied and immediately took charge.

"David, you and Mr. Slate get out from underfoot and go into the parlour until I call you for lunch. Richard, if you will follow Becca she will show you and the luggage to the appropriate rooms. Mrs. Slate, if you will assist me I think we can feed this crew in short order."

The group enjoyed a hearty soup and sandwich lunch and by the time tea and pie were being served they were all on a first name basis. Becca delivered her dishes to the sink and glanced out the kitchen window. It was still snowing heavily.

"Sorry folks but I am going to have to leave. I need to get my stuff home before it's buried in the back of the truck."

"I can give you a hand," said her father.

"No you can't," said Mary, "not with that knee."

"I'll help," offered Richard.

"Mum's right, Dad. I need a helper with two good legs. Thanks Richard. Let's go!"

†

Even with snow tires and chains on her pickup Becca had to fight her way along the snow-choked concession to her farm. On the way she explained to Richard the Stone family cooperative.

The home farm belonged to her parents. Next to it, on the south side, was her brother Paul's farm where he, his wife Susan and their daughter Carol lived. Becca's farm was on the north side, where the farmhouse served as her home, office and treatment area for her small animal practice. Part of the barn was devoted to her large animal patients and the rest to regular farm use. She didn't farm the land, but her father and brother did, with one hired man, Tom Miller, who lived with his family in Udney. It was a profitable partnership. Thankfully Tom had finished plowing the lane and when they pulled up to her barn he was working on the paths. Becca introduced him and with his help they quickly unloaded her goods.

"Thanks for your help Rick, I really didn't want my father to come over here."

"Why?"

"C'mon, I'll show you." Becca led him into the barn, where only two stalls were occupied. As the humans approached, the residents began to stir, nodding their heads and shaking their manes in welcome.

"They're magnificent!" exclaimed Richard.

'They' were a matched pair of Clydesdale heavy horses. Under the barn lights their glossy coats shone like burnished bronze, emphasizing the pure white blazes on their foreheads and the ebony manes cascading from their powerful necks.

"Are they yours?"

Becca reached out, stroked the nose of the nearest and smiled.

"No, they are a Christmas gift for my father. The Stones have always kept heavy horses for work and pleasure. My Dad had a championship team, Atlas and Hercules. He doted on them. Sadly old age and ill health forced him to put them down last summer. He misses them dearly, so my brother Paul, Mum and I decided to surprise him with these guys. They are two year old brothers from the same bloodline as Atlas and Hercules. Now you know why I had to keep Dad away until Christmas."

Richard reached tentatively toward the other horse's muzzle.

"Go ahead," said Becca.

He gently touched and began to stroke softly. The young horse nodded his head in response and then rolled back his upper lip.

"He smiled at me!"

"Well, not really," responded Becca, "but just like people he likes the attention."

She glanced at her watch. "We had better go. I have to change before we head back for dinner."

†

After outfitting Alexander in some of Dave's casual clothes Mary dismissed both from the house to the barn to do man stuff.

She had taken an immediate liking to Isabelle Slate. Chatting over a second cup of tea she learned Isabelle had been born and raised on a farm in Saskatchewan, met and married Alex there and moved to Toronto where she now kept a large home and volunteered at their church, while her husband spent much of his time traveling on CPR business. Richard was their only child. It was clear Richard was the couple's pride and joy, but Mary sensed some tension in the father and son relationship. The elder Slate had wanted his son to follow in his footsteps and started him right out of high school in a CPR office, to learn the business. Richard had other ideas. After a year of shuffling paper and scheduling freight he had announced his desire to become a teacher, left the CPR and enrolled in the Toronto Normal School. His father had not been pleased. But Richard had excelled, was set to graduate in the spring and hoped to begin his teaching career in the next school year.

Isabelle explained, "Alexander has been under a lot of pressure for the last three years to reorganize CP's freight handling systems and he has been very tense and all business of late. I'm not even sure he realizes it's Christmas! Richard and I decided to take this business trip with him so the three of us could have some holiday time together. So far it has not worked out well. Perhaps this stopover will stir some Christmas spirit."

"Maybe I can help you with that," said Mary. "My son Paul, his wife Susan and my granddaughter Carol live on the farm next door. Every year on Christmas Eve, Paul and David deliver Christmas parcels to the less fortunate families in our community. The United Church Women rely on me to organize the white gifts and other needed items for the trip. Would you like to help?"

Isabelle placed her cup on the saucer and smiled. "Show me what to do."

†

Dave was pleased to escape to his farm office in the barn. It was his sanctuary and comfort zone. It was where he and other men from the community often gathered to discuss matters of importance, from politics to farming, and of course hockey. It featured a small potbellied stove, a desk with a radio, and a collection of mismatched wooden chairs. Alexander Slate stood surveying the pictures, newspaper clippings and ribbons posted on the walls. An oil painting of a team of Clydesdale horses, in harness to a sleigh, was the centre piece.

"A handsome pair," commented Slate, "and a winning team too."

"Atlas and Hercules were the best heavy horses in the area for more than a decade. They died this past summer." He glanced toward the empty stalls. "I miss them."

"I am sorry for your loss. But just like the steam locomotives in my world, their time had passed. I loved the sound and fury of those great machines and rue their passing. But the new diesels are more efficient and powerful. They move more freight faster. That is why we need to eliminate the milk runs and multiple stops at stations like yours in Udney. The meetings I am attending in Winnipeg will be addressing that issue."

"Alex, there is always more than first meets the eye when planning change. Those horses were an important part of our community and part of a tradition that speaks to what country life is all about. I miss them especially tonight, because I would be preparing them for the annual Christmas cheer run to deliver food and gifts to the less fortunate families in our community. They pulled a sleigh loaded with holiday treats that my son Paul and I would deliver to local farms."

"Is that really necessary?"

"Indeed it is. Alex, did you see the partially built structure behind the church that we passed on our way from the station? It's our new Community Centre."

"I did. What's holding up construction?"

"Money for materials. We have lots of volunteer labour and should be working, even in the winter, but most local families are strapped for cash, so we raise what we can and build as we go. That is what community is all about. We have about seventy farms in our community and we depend on each other. That's why your comment about closing the Udney station worries me. That station is one of the anchors of our community. The church is the other and we really need that community centre; even more now, because we have just lost our school."

"I see," answered Slate, "but time marches on and sometimes traditions get left behind."

"Not all I hope," said Dave. He checked his watch.

"We had better get back to the house and see what the women have planned for dinner."

†

"That was delicious, Mrs. Stone. I travel so much I seldom get a home cooked meal. Thank you."

"Please call me Mary, and your Isabelle deserves much of the credit. She prepared the vegetables and her recipe for mashed carrots is definitely going into my book. We combined forces on the pie as a test run for tomorrow's baking for the church supper and I must say we had fun doing it."

She turned to her husband. "David, Paul called to see if your leg will be up to making the community gift run tomorrow."

"I wouldn't miss it, and Alex has volunteered to help. The weather report said the snow will keep up so it looks like Thor and Odin will be pressed into service this year and we will be using his cutter."

"Thanks Alex. Isabelle has been helping me too. We had fun assembling parcels this afternoon and we expect to finish wrapping presents tonight. You two men can listen to the hockey game on the radio and between periods ready our work for loading. Tomorrow morning, once you men are out from underfoot and on the road, Isabelle and I will start on the pies for the supper."

"You two make quite a team Mum," said Becca, "so... if Mrs. Slate is helping you tomorrow does that mean I am off the hook for pie filling?"

Mary smiled, "Looks like it."

"Great! And it's just as well. I already have two dogs boarding over the holidays, two more arriving tomorrow and a very sick cat in the clinic. I have to sort and shelve the supplies that I picked up today and I have visits scheduled to the Rimkay and Hunter farms to inoculate stock. And don't forget I am hosting the family for treats, before we leave for the church supper and service."

Becca nodded toward Richard.

"Richard has offered his help hold the fort at the clinic while I'm on the road so you two will have the house to yourselves."

The ringing of the wooden telephone box on the wall interrupted the conversation. Mary lifted the receiver from the cradle, placed it to her ear and spoke into the trumpet.

"Hello... yes, she's here Gail, just a minute, I'll put her on. Becca, it's Gail Wilson."

"Yes Mrs. Wilson, I understand. What are the roads like over your way? Can I get my truck into your yard? Good. I will be there as soon as I can."

"Sorry folks, I have to go. The Wilson's dairy cow has gone into labour and she is having problems. Gail's husband Bill is away working with the CPR crew and she needs my help."

Dave spoke up, " It's still bad out there. You shouldn't go alone."

"She won't have to. I'll go with her," said Richard.

"Offer accepted," said Becca. "Let's go."

†

Richard opened and held the small entry door for Becca and her birthing kit then followed her into the Wilson's barn. Gail Wilson was standing near an open stall awaiting them. Becca greeted her and introduced him.

When Becca entered the stall she saw that Daisy was down on her side in the straw and clearly in distress. The cow's head was turned and her neck strained as she tried to reach toward her hindquarters. Becca knelt and stroked her muzzle.

"It's okay, girl. Let's see if I can help you."

Daisy's huge brown eyes rolled in response and she lowed pitifully, confirming her unease.

"Gail, how long has she been in labour?"

"About three hours, Dr. Stone. Bill was worried there might be a problem. When he examined her this morning before he left to work with the derailment crew he was concerned that the calf had not yet turned."

Becca moved her hands down Daisy's body and traced the outline of the unborn calf in her belly. Her examination confirmed what Bill suspected.

"Well, Bill was right; the calf still hasn't turned and isn't presenting for delivery. I am afraid Daisy is facing a breech birth."

"What's wrong?" asked Richard.

Becca opened her birthing kit and removed a large tub of lanolin cream. After rolling up her right sleeve to her shoulder she smeared the lanolin on her hand and arm. While doing so she explained.

"The calf is stuck sideways in Daisy's womb. She needs our help before she can deliver naturally. Gail, please hold her head and comfort her. Richard..."

"Who, me?"

"Yes, you. I need you to hold her hind leg wide and keep her from kicking me."

Richard took his place and gingerly grasped Daisy's left hind leg.

"Don't be tentative. Hold it tightly and well spread."

Becca knelt and carefully inserted her hand and then her arm into the cow's womb, seeking the calf's front legs. She punctured the amniotic sac and found them and using them for leverage began to roll and turn the unborn calf's body. It was not easy and Daisy lowed in distress as Becca strained to accomplish the repositioning. Finally she was able to find the head and after carefully freeing the umbilical cord had the calf in position for Daisy to deliver on her own.

Daisy responded immediately; the muscles in her hindquarters strained and in a rush of fluid the calf slipped out onto the straw. It was a heifer.

Becca motioned to Richard to release her leg. The threesome backed away slowly and closed the stall door. Now it was up to Daisy.

For a moment she seemed surprised to find this new creature in her stall, but instinct prevailed and she began to clean her baby with strokes of her huge pink tongue. The group stood talking softly, watching mother and calf interact and waiting for the next step in the birth cycle. It was soon in coming.

The little heifer began struggling to stand. Once, twice... she tried so hard; but the initial efforts ended in an undignified collapse into a tangle of spindly legs. Daisy lowed and the calf tried again and again, until finally she stayed standing on all fours, gazing around at her strange new world. But not for long. Soon instinct and hunger had her snuffling between her mother's legs, seeking her first meal. Daisy accepted this new sensation calmly. Standing stock still, she turned her head and began to nuzzle and caress her calf.

"Thanks Dr. Stone, I think I can handle things from here."

"I am sure you can Gail. Have you heard from your husband? How is the track repair coming?"

"Bill called from the yard in Washago. He said it was still a terrible mess and the weather isn't helping. He won't be home until they finish and that may not be until late Christmas Day."

†

The concession road remained unplowed but Becca's faithful Ford fought its way slowly through the fresh snow toward home.

"That was incredible Becca. Do you have to do that often?"

"No, most of my large animal work is inoculations, dental and lately insemination."

"Well, tonight's adventure has given me a terrific story to tell my students, and perhaps some lessons as well."

"Have you decided where you want to teach?"

"Not exactly, but it won't be in Toronto. If I stayed there I would have to live at home. I want to get out on my own. Besides they tell us that rural communities are very short of teachers, especially men. Is there a school in Udney?"

"There is, but it's closing. They're building a larger school in Brechin, a few miles from here. It opens this September. My Mum is on the Board."

Becca turned into her parents' driveway. It too needed plowing again and to reach the drive-yard she had to follow the tracks they had made on the way out.

"Well, here's home. Given the weather and the status of the track repairs I don't think you will be leaving any time soon. Do you still want to help me tomorrow?"

Richard smiled, "You bet! I wouldn't mind at all if we had to stay here for Christmas. I have really enjoyed meeting your family and..." —Richard moved a little closer and leaned toward Becca—"and you." Suddenly the cab of the Ford was flooded with light. Tom Miller had arrived on the tractor to plow.

†

The morning of December twenty fourth presented a mix of weather. Snow flurries alternated with periods of bright sunlight. It would be a perfect day for delivering the Christmas packages. Dave, Richard and Alex piled the Christmas cheer parcels on the back porch and retreated to the kitchen to join the women for tea while they waited for Paul. Sixteen year old Shep's valiant woofing from his rug by the McClary alerted them to the team's arrival and the men pulled on their coats and boots and went to greet them. Paul had brought the cutter to a stop near the rear of the house and Thor and Odin were showing their eagerness to start the journey by nodding their heads and stamping their feathered hooves in anticipation of a good run. Mary and Isabelle put down their tea mugs and went outside to join the men. Paul and Dave were already loading the parcels and Alex and Richard were in the sleigh helping to store them.

"Alright Stone family and friends," said Mary, "it is time to get organized. Dave, you, Paul and Alex will have a long day. Once you leave here, your first stop will be to drop Richard off at Becca's. Then go to the railway station to pick up the donations Charlie Graham has collected. Next deliver your whole load to the church. As usual Reverend Campbell and his volunteers will repack the items into lots for each family. Once you have the list of recipients you can plan your route. Remember, you need to be back here well before dark to get cleaned up and take us over to Becca's for her reception, before we go to the church. So don't waste time talking horses and hockey and sampling new batches of holiday cheer at every stop." Dave smiled at this annual admonition.

"No problem dear, this year we have Alex to keep us on track."

With that he joined Paul and the others aboard the cutter; Paul called up the horses and they were on their way.

†

Becca was pleased. By some miracle of organization and luck the whole Stone family and their guests had made it to her house on time. The snowfall had lessened considerably and she had been able to complete her rounds quickly. Richard had done an admirable job of caring for the clinic and taking in the arriving animals for board. She had picked up her mother and Isabelle with the party goodies on her way home and between the four of them everything was in place when Dave, Alex, Paul, Susan and her little niece Carol arrived in the cutter. Becca had prepared both regular and "special" bowls of eggnog to complement the baked treats and spirits were high. The Slates had donned their traveling clothes for church and the Stones too were ready for the service. They would all leave straight from Becca's. It had been a good day for the men on the Christmas cheer run and even Alex had gotten into the spirit of things.

"I was surprised at your community's generosity, and I must say that arriving by horse and sleigh made us quite the celebrities. I will forever remember the looks on the children's faces when they saw the presents; and the genuine words of thanks from the parents for the kindness of their neighbours. It reminded me of what Christmas is all about."

Becca interrupted and asked for everyone's attention.

"We have to leave for church soon, but I need Dad's opinion on something before we go. Dad do you think you could hobble down to the barn to check out some stock?"

"Give me my coat and cane and let's go."

Paul joined them and the threesome entered the barn through the side door near the stalls. Becca turned on the lights.

The duo of Clydesdale colts stood like bronze statues, golden brown coats gleaming, beautifully offset by their ebony manes. They began to stir, stamping their hooves and nodding their heads in greeting. Dave was speechless. He began to move toward them. Then turned, to find the entire group gathered behind him.

Little Carol pointed and announced, "Santa brought Grampa some new horses!"

"Merry Christmas Dad!" said Becca and Paul.

Dave smiled. His eyes sparkled, but he could not speak. He nodded and then turned and greeted his new "boys" with muzzle rubs and gentle words only they could hear.

†

Leaving Dave and his new team to bond, the group retreated to Becca's parlour to clean up and prepare for church. Then the telephone rang.

"Oh no," said Mary. "I hope that's not a duty call for you, Becca."

Becca shrugged and answered the telephone.

"Hello ... Yes, he's here. I'll put him on."

"Mr. Slate, it's Charlie Graham, for you."

"Alexander Slate speaking. Yes. I understand, station-master. Please have my crew informed and ask them to prepare for immediate departure. We will be there shortly."

Alexander Slate explained the call. "The track has been reopened. The engine that will haul our car to Winnipeg is waiting for us at Washago. I am sorry to say, we must leave immediately."

Mary as usual took over.

"I'm sorry too. I was looking forward to sharing the supper and service with you all; but it can't be helped. Paul, please go the barn and collect your father. Becca, would you drive Richard to our house to get the Slate's bags? If you leave right away you can meet us at the station. Isabelle, could I ask you to help me ..."

Mary turned to see the Slates having a private conversation. Alexander spoke first.

"Becca, may I use your office for a moment?"

"Certainly Mr. Slate, but please excuse the mess."

"And I will give your mum a hand with the clean up," added Isabelle.

"Suits me," replied Becca. "Come on Rick, let's get going."

†

The Udney station was a hive of activity. Snow was still falling lightly and the flakes danced in the glow of the platform lights. The train crew had restarted the engine and the streamliner once again rumbled with power.

The Stone family and Alexander and Isabelle Slate had gathered in the brightly lit waiting room where the woodstove in the corner was doing its best to ward off winter's chill. Station-master Graham was addressing the gathering.

"Thank you, Mr. Slate. The credit goes to our CPR emergency repair crews, with a big assist to the local men who provided the extra labour."

"Where are Becca and Richard?" asked Dave.

"I think I saw headlights pulling into the parking lot a few minutes ago," said Paul.

Mary Stone knew that. She had been watching out the rear window when Becca's truck pulled in. She had also seen the couple exit the truck and pause, silhouetted by the yard light, to share a private goodbye.

"I'll go and see," offered Paul.

"No Paul, stay here," said his mother.

Isabelle, too, had been watching out the window; the two mothers exchanged knowing looks.

"Yes," added Isabelle, "I am certain they will be here in a minute."

The staccato blast of the streamliner's horn punctuated her comment.

"That's the call to board," said Alexander. "Come Isabelle, we must leave now in order to make our connection."

The group exited the station and gathered near the passenger car. Becca and Richard joined them, carrying the bags between them.

"It's about time you two got here," grinned Paul. "What took you?"

The pair smiled at each other. "Mind your own business brother."

"Goodbye Isabelle, Alex," Dave said. He nodded toward their son, "And you too Richard. It was a pleasure meeting you all."

"Indeed," said Mary. "You added some excitement to our Christmas and we thank you for your help in spreading the holiday spirit in Udney."

"It is us who should be thanking you," responded Isabelle. "You are a terrific hostess Mary, and you have a wonderful family. Merry Christmas!" She hugged Mary and then Becca.

"Come Richard, we must go." They boarded.

Alexander Slate paused at the bottom of the steps. He had resumed his business demeanour.

"Mr. Stone, I agree with my wife. The Slate family and the CPR owe you and this community a debt of gratitude for your kindness and support. It has been appreciated." He extended his hand, the two locked eyes, smiled and then shook firmly.

"And enjoy your Christmas gift, Dave."

Then he removed an envelope from his breast pocket and handed it to Mary.

"Merry Christmas!"

He turned quickly and boarded, followed by the conductor who secured the door. Following another blast of the horn the rumble of the diesel engines became a roar and the train pulled slowly away, its rear lights disappearing behind the curtain of falling snow.

†

The entire Stone family had managed to fit itself into Paul's cutter for the trip to church. Paul and Dave were on the driver's bench with Carol wedged between them, and Mary sat in the back flanked by Becca and Susan. The horses pulled away with a will and Paul guided the sleigh onto the concession road. The snow had stopped and left the landscape wrapped in a mantle of white which reflected the lustre of the stars twinkling above. They could see the steeple of the Udney United Church shining in the distance. It was a perfect Christmas Eve.

Mary examined the envelope in her hand. It was addressed to the Stone Family. She opened it, paused, and then read aloud.

Dear Stone Family,

Thank you for your hospitality at this special time of year and most of all for reminding me of what helping others, both personally and as a community, adds to the quality of our lives. You have demonstrated in word and deed the importance of maintaining the traditions and customs that have built strong families, good communities and our great country. Progress brings change and CPR will have to close many of its small depots, but you can be assured that as long as I have a say, the trains will still stop in Udney.

Alexander Slate.

"That is great news!" said Dave.

"There's more," said Mary.

"It's a cheque," chimed in Becca.

"A cheque?" queried Paul.

"It is made out to the Udney Community Centre, in the amount of $1,000.00."

"Wow!" exclaimed Paul. "Merry Christmas indeed, and a very happy New Year too!"

"Speaking of the new year, Mum," asked Becca, "will they be needing more teachers for the new school in Brechin?"

"Yes, I expect they will."

"Will you be on the hiring committee?"

"Probably. Why do you ask, dear?"

The colour that rose in Becca's cheeks was not just from the cold.

"Aah ... just wondering. You never know what or whom the new year might bring to our community and our next Christmas."

Her comment was punctuated by the sound of church bells ringing joyously in the crisp winter air, calling them to join their community in celebrating the wonder and joy of Christmas.

About the Author

To supplement the information in the foreword, preface and dedication, there is some special "karma" I wish to share with you.

My wife Carol is a leading character in many of my stories and of course her December 25th birth date contributes much to the context and drama of the Christmas stories; but there is another connection between us, which adds a unique facet to my storytelling.

Carol and I were born in the same year (194...) in the same hospital (Toronto Western) just five days apart; she, on Christmas Day the 25th and I on the 30th of December. *As a result we actually spent our first Christmas together in the hospital nursery over sixty years ago. I claim to this day that as the older woman she took advantage and set me up for marriage twenty years later.* Was it just luck, or fate that brought and kept us together? Who knows? But we believe it was the "magic" of Christmas, and after reading these stories we think you might agree.

We grew up in communities far distant, but met again by chance at age seventeen and have been together sharing life's trials and triumphs ever since. We are proud to have raised two wonderful children, son Rob and daughter Dana, and to have contributed to organizing or working with many organizations in our community. Carol and I now live in Severn Township near Orillia, Ontario where we enjoy our summers playing golf and cruising in our 1968 Mustang and our winters in Arizona in our home at Roadrunner Lake.

Until my late forties I was known as a storyteller, but I seldom wrote those tales down. However, when I retired after thirty five years as an educator (teacher, principal and Director of Education) I decided to try and write stories about the exceptional events and wonderful people that had enriched our lives. Drawing on my experiences, I strove to recreate the emotion and impact of those special moments in life that touch us all. I am fortunate to have had some success and thankful to have been able to share my tales in many ways.

Publication Credits

I wish to recognize and thank the following sources that have published my short stories and plays:

Magazines: *Reminisce, Good Old Days, Capper's, New Moon Network, The Front Porch* and *Lake Simcoe Living.*

Christmas Special Edition Books: *Reminisce* and *Good Old Days*

Daily Newspaper Christmas Serials: *Orillia Packet and Times* and other Sun Media publications for nine consecutive years.

Mainstream Anthologies: *Chicken Soup for the Soul: Christmas,* 2007; *Fathers and Sons,* 2008; *True Love,* 2009; *Oh Canada,* 2011; *Married Life,* 2012; *Hooked on Hockey,* 2012. Adams Media: *A Cup of Comfort For Inspiration,* 2003; *My Teacher Is My Hero,* 2008; *For A Better World,* 2010.

Limited Edition Anthologies: *Our Literary Lapses,* 2009; *From The Cottage Porch,* 2011; *A Canvas of Words,* 2011.

Interactive Theatre: "Rodeo Round-Up" and "Last Kiss"; plays written for and performed at Roadrunner Lake Resort in Scottsdale Arizona.

Single Author Anthologies: *Angels, Stars and Trees: Tales of Christmas Magic* (Scrivener Press, 2007); *Home For Christmas* (Scrivener Press, 2012).

My work has also aired on CBC Radio One's First Person Singular and won first place in competitions held by *The Toronto Sun, The Orillia Packet and Times* and *The Owen Sound Sun Times.*